EVERY ARC BENDS ITS RADIAN

A NOVEL

SERGIO DE LA PAVA

SIMON & SCHUSTER

NEW YORK LONDON TORONTO SYDNEY NEW DELHI

100 YEARS

SIMON & SCHUSTER

Simon & Schuster
1230 Avenue of the Americas
New York, NY 10020

First Simon & Schuster hardcover edition November 2024

SIMON & SCHUSTER and colophon are registered trademarks of Simon & Schuster, LLC

Simon & Schuster: Celebrating 100 Years of Publishing in 2024

For information about special discounts for bulk purchases, please contact Simon & Schuster Special Sales at 1-866-506-1949 or business@simonandschuster.com.

The Simon & Schuster Speakers Bureau can bring authors to your live event. For more information or to book an event, contact the Simon & Schuster Speakers Bureau at 1-866-248-3049 or visit our website at www.simonspeakers.com.

Interior design by Carly Loman

Manufactured in the United States of America

1   3   5   7   9   10   8   6   4   2

Library of Congress Cataloging-in-Publication Data is available.

ISBN 978-1-6680-5670-7
ISBN 978-1-6680-5672-1 (ebook)

Para Claudia

El preámbulo de la muerte no es ni el nacimiento ni la vida, es el sueño. El ser humano debería vivir eternamente aterrorizado por la posibilidad de despertar a una pesadilla.

—Unknown *in conversation*

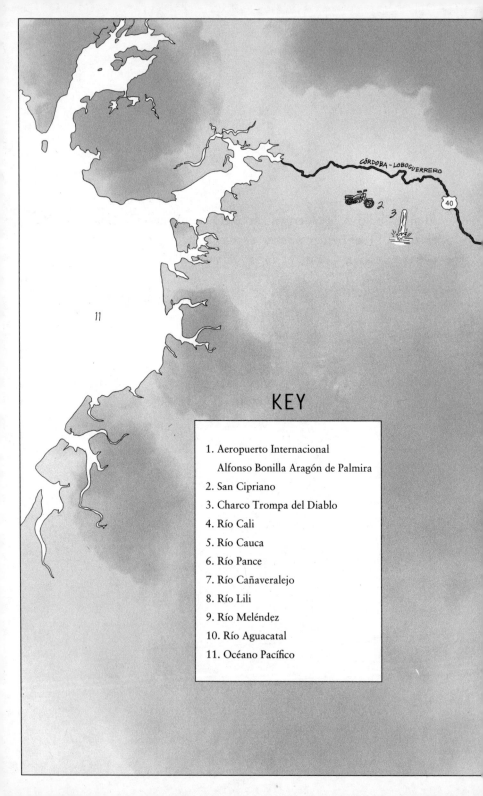

CÓRDOBA - LOBOGUERRERO

40

11

2 3

KEY

1. Aeropuerto Internacional
   Alfonso Bonilla Aragón de Palmira
2. San Cipriano
3. Charco Trompa del Diablo
4. Río Cali
5. Río Cauca
6. Río Pance
7. Río Cañaveralejo
8. Río Lili
9. Río Meléndez
10. Río Aguacatal
11. Océano Pacífico

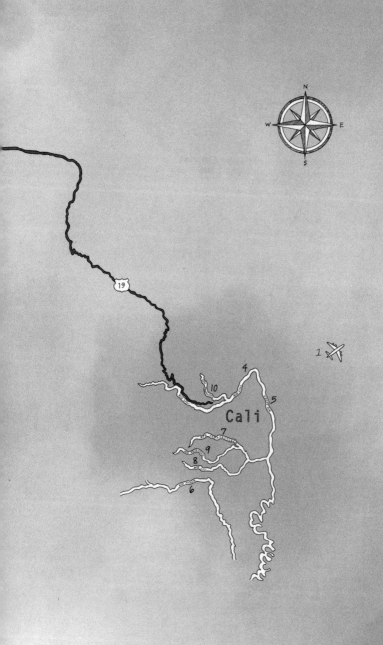

KEY

1. Ciudad Jardín
2. Parque de la Babilla
3. Parque el Gato de Tejada
4. Torre de Cali
5. Bichacue Yath Arte y Naturaleza
6. Cristo Rey
7. Cerro de las Tres Cruces
8. Estatua Sebastían de Belalcázar
9. Zoológico de Cali
10. La Buitrera
11. Iglesia la Ermita
12. Parque de los Poetas

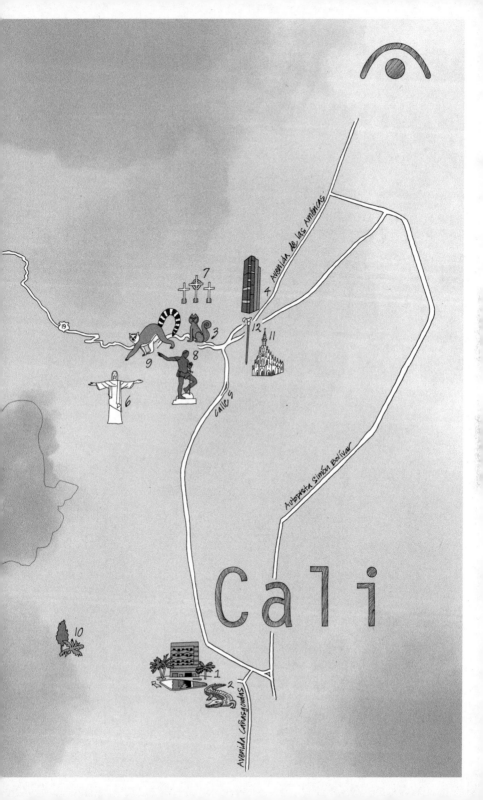

EVERY ARC BENDS ITS RADIAN

ONE

1st entry: a light alight

THE ARGUMENT

A man responds to horror with flight. But evasion and connection are bipolar.

That was about the time I put my faith in nothing.

I don't mean to say there wasn't anything I put my faith in. I'm asserting something like the opposite. Because, above all, I had acted. The action was placing all my dwindling faith in a very particular entity, and that entity was the referent we invoke whenever we form the word *Nothing*.

Thing about doing that is the freedom. But is freedom even a good? Nothing begets nothing and that includes no restrictions. If you expand outward what you might do, with little regard for notions like precedent or consequence, the result can be a kind of drive to negation. Seeing what I'd seen in my debtors' prison of an apartment? Man, there was nothing I wouldn't do after that.

So, Colombia?

Even just buying the plane ticket my head's already in Spanish. So when I choose nonrefundable to save money I recall how, growing up, my sister Genevieve and I would call cash *effective* in deference to the brilliant Spanish-speaking maniacs who looked at that damned force and decided that only the word *efectivo* could do it justice. And I'm relying mostly on third-party observation here, but when it comes to cash, inventions don't come any more effective.

Cartagena is my initial thought, but further reflection results in Cali, Colombia, instead. Because I don't need a historic walled city right now, I need a descent into simple instinct. And forgive me, Jane, but this is the magic potion I'm going to ingest in hopes of erasing all this.

The airport in Cali. It's been an era since I've been, so the sight of so many authorized machine guns unsettles at first.

Now the minimally nice woman in customs wants to know the purpose of my trip, and when I say the purpose is «amnesia» I know immediately that's a mistake. But instead of fixing it I make it worse when I can't answer an even simpler question: *Where are you going?*

Where am I going?

She means *¿hotel o familia?* but I'm off on the deeper question.

Her voice doesn't help. All Colombian women talk the same way and it's magical. Couple syllables and I'm two feet tall in Jersey City and it's okay to not understand anything that's happening because any one of those many angelic voices can individually make everything all right.

Back in the urgent here and now, Colombia doesn't want to let me in. My answers are satisfying no one. And things are maybe starting to escalate in the special way that place has, when I remember Cousin Mauro. Mauro, who months ago called to no response but who will still be a *missed call* on my phone so I can change my story for at least the third time to one where that is who I will be staying with. Only I've misplaced the address, one of those Colombian postal messes with the Valle del Maracuyá fucking Diagonal Norte whatever the fuck.

No one official takes kindly to this latest flourish, but I'm ignoring them and dialing and before anyone really knows what's happened I've got Mauro on the line and am *reminding* him of my arrival and how I need his address so that the fine folks at Aeropuerto Internacional Alfonso Bonilla Aragón de Palmira with the palm trees and lithe women and ungodly humidity and gleeful yelps can verify that I will not be an undomiciled ward of the state wandering the streets of Cali without aim.

It works. If you need to improv into any kind of confidence operation, this particular *primo* of mine is your man.

Later, at the hotel in *Ciudad Jardín*, picked on the recommendation of a taxi driver whose middle name somehow features a strange symbol ⌐• that I swear an argument could be made is subtly formed by the official Colombian stamp on my passport, the full implication of my rashness hits me.

I had intended a kind of . . . I don't know what I'd intended. I was running. Away or to or from, I didn't know. But all that depended on invisibility and instead here's my phone blowing up with disbelief that I'm in *jueputa Cali, mijo*. Also the realization, as I look out the window and listen to the messages, that I have come to Cali, Colombia, seeking solitude during its annual post-Christmas, end-of-the-year *Feria de Cali*, which is like Rio de Janeiro's *Carnaval*, only fun.

Tomorrow I'll claim jet lag and tomorrow I'll worry about how I'm going to pay for this loft in what is a pretty fucking killer hotel. Tonight we drink.

Only there's no *we*. Drink, thankfully, there is. And is. Until one of those voices again and:

—*Hay, mi amor, estamos cerrados.*

Yes, I say. I'm all wit when fueled by *aguardiente*, man. We're *all* closed.

2nd entry: permanence

THE ARGUMENT

A desperate woman conceives of a possible solution.

Next day's night Mauro is running through a series of options for the rest of the evening. And I'm not saying yes to any of them but not exactly no either, and the more and more *aguardiente*, the tougher to keep up the politeness. Truth is, kinetic activity builds organically around us until leaving that impromptu family reunion would be impossible anyway.

Part of that is my aunt Fanny. During one of those natural lulls where I'm free to be quiet, I stare at her undetected. How old is she? Nineties? I see her hanging in our American living room, some medical contraption making her a marionette. More than three decades ago now. Hanging from that doorframe before immigration machinations send her back to Colombia and the woman I'm looking at now is the same woman, the same face. Nothing about the face is the same except everything. What's in a face so persists that all Time's damage cannot erase it entirely?

And Mauro picks that moment, with my head diffused in a cloud, to introduce a foreign element he's been teasing all night.

"About dah favor, *primo*." All day he's giving me English and I'm in Spanish, like we've silently agreed to not be at our best.

—Unless the favor is for me to black out drunk, what shame, but I will have to say no.

"Remember Doña Carlotta?"

—The words, not so much the person. ¿She wore those fancy headscarves? ¡In this ungodly heat!

No, apparently that was the original Carlotta, this is her daughter.

Either way, seems she's requested a meeting with me, the improbability of which starts to hit me hard as I learn that Mauro, ever helpful, has already accepted on my behalf. So that will happen tomorrow.

A tragedy, really, he says, and everyone around us nods in agreement.

I nod too, which in my complete ignorance of the tragic contours makes no sense at all.

But still.

3rd entry: all that is the case

THE ARGUMENT

The problem is introduced. Interrogated from more than one angle is not just its potential solubility but also whether the party being courted is even in position to help.

Waking life in Cali, for me, has many dreamlike qualities. So opening my eyes isn't clearly a return to reality from imagination. And the two little girls staring at me in concert are like guides betwixt the two worlds. They're relatives, I know that much, but before I can even begin to investigate they giggle and run away.

Mauro replaces them and is apologetic but also thinks I shouldn't keep the latest Doña Carlotta waiting any longer. I have an unfortunate quality that no matter how much I drink I still remember everything. But remembering is not the same as understanding and all this makes even less sense than it did the night before.

—¿What does this treat of?

"Is about her daughter."

He hands me something that he says will help, but when I study the saucer and cup it's tea. Am I in fucking Okinawa? Where's the black tar *tinto*, man? I keep this to myself and walk into a room that's half indoors, half outdoors, with one of those prototypically Colombian tile floors.

The woman is familiar. But I can't tell if it's specific or just the type. In the air is not exactly grief, but a kind of defeated anxiety that's ready to activate into grief at any second. She almost smiles, says she remembers me. Is she saying she recognizes me? Unclear, but apparently her mother would tell how when I was maybe four, I would break rooms up by announcing I was starting to get angry. And now look at my grays.

She says she can't believe this is my first time back, and I don't correct her that I was back at eight, twenty, and twenty-four but that, yes, it's been a long time.

Carlotta has heard a lot about me, she says, but most of it confusing. Was I a poet? A philosopher?

Was I? Some lines a few times in magazines with circulation in the teens. Unceremoniously ejected two classes shy.

But aren't I now *un ojo privado*, words I'd never before heard in that combination so that I almost laughed.

—¿I guess I'm like a poet/philosopher/private eye?

—¿Is that a good job in the States?

—It's a weird country.

At any rate it's the last part of my occupation she's interested in. She takes a deep breath and I notice she's holding a rosary.

—Oh, my son. I used to say, I like to say, that Angelica is my *gringa* daughter. She was our only, our baby. A uterine miracle from God and medicine. Her education was bilingual, we had more money by then. Her father, my husband, was a very pre-pared man. A medical doctor. He died ten years ago when she was twelve. A stroke they said. But I persevered. She was my life. The rest . . .

She stops and suddenly it's as if a censor has entered the room.

—¿What came to pass? —is all I can manage.

—I would prefer to know with certitude that she is dead than some of the things living in my mind. The mental life. That's where true suffering is. The body is nothing in comparison.

—¿When did you last see her?

—Four days. Four days that have landed on my soul like the forty Jesus spent in the desert with Satan. The day after my birthday, a great reunion then this.

—¿This a picture of her?

—Si, mi amor.

It's an odd photo to have framed. Certainly not professionally done. And full of peculiar lighting and angles. But also the face. Her daughter was an extremely beautiful woman with decidedly eerie, maybe unattractive, features. I want to explore the eeriness but the beauty won't allow it.

—¿What do the police say?

—¿What are they going to say? If they're pure garbage.

—¿Where's her boyfriend these days?

—She doesn't have one. ¿See? A sound girl. A genius. A cerebrum. MIT. You're from the States, you know what MIT means. ¿From where did you graduate?

—From Rutgers I didn't.

—¿What's that?

—Precisely. So this is a good time for me to ask how you think I can help.

—Find her, find my Angelica.

—¿How?

—You're a detective.

—A private detective, not even an especially good one.

—God sent you, many orations.

—No, he would have sent someone better. I mostly take pictures of cheap men leaving cheap hotel rooms.

—¿If she dies, what will they say about those who rejected my pleas for help? I have money.

Peripheral vision, a strength. Mauro is nodding greedily.

—You'll need it —I say.

—You can have all that's mine.

—No, for whoever you get and the bribes he's going to have to pay.

But people get things in their heads, man, things they shouldn't. Like this idea that I'm heaven-sent and her only hope. So we go on like that until I just surrender to it all with instructions to take me to her house and Angelica's room within, and also to write down a list of things I'll need.

Truth is, I'm starting to think I may never go back. May not *return stateside* is how I put it mentally to make it seem more dramatic.

That and I can probably find a dead body as well as the next guy.

4th entry: she's only sleeping

THE ARGUMENT

The indeterminacy of just Everything is what gets you.

Rooting around a dead woman's room, what a way to make a living. The only thing worse is not making one.

She wasn't kidding about having money, my only client. Not if the house is any indication.

No cellphone anywhere is a potential positive sign, no? Not a huge deal, just that finding her phone would portend almost certain death, the only event left that can reliably separate privileged humanity from their devices.

So no device of any kind in the room feels like planning, and I start to adjust my pessimism downward.

Downstairs, in the living room, like a museum depicting long ago opulence.

—¿What's her boyfriend's name again?

—I told you, she doesn't have one.

—¿If she did, who would it be?

—I don't understand.

—¿Who's her closest female friend?

—No one, she doesn't, she . . .

This should surprise me more than it does, but I was already getting that distinct feeling.

—This is a very nice house.

—Thank you, Rivilerto, I decorated it myself.

"It's Riv."

—*¿Reev?* ¿Qué es eso?

—Es mi nombre, Riv.

—¿A que horas?

"At all hours, from birth certificate on."

—¿No Rivilerto?

—No.

—¿No Rivilerto del Rio?

—del Rio, yes. But Riv, not that thing you're saying.

—¿And Riv is short for?

—Nothing, you are hearing it in all its extended glory.

—Uy.

—Anyway, you have expensive taste.

—Hmm.

—Maybe everyone does. Difference is you get to feed yours. ¿How come?

—¿How so, *how*?

—¿How have you paid for all this?

—¡You insult me!

—Not intentionally.

—Apology accepted.

—I'm more interested in the answer.

—¿To what?

—¿To how you pay for all this?

—I told you my husband was a doctor. ¿Do you not listen to me when I speak? ¿Is it because I'm a woman? ¿Are you a sexist?

—Yes, I'm a sexist. I believe the female sex is superior. As far as being a doctor, there must be a lot of well-heeled sick people around here to cover all this.

—He was a healer, he was loved.

—¿By all? ¿Is there anyone, or anyones, he failed to heal who maybe took it personally?

—No one, of course.

—¿What about Angelica? You say she had no friends. ¿Anyone most not her friend?

—I didn't say she had no friends. She was a young lady of the house, of that ambience.

—Sure but . . .

—Her studies, her work, is what mattered to her. I'm sure in the States . . . she kept to herself. She'd only been back less than a year.

—¿What do you mean when you say her studies, her work? ¿What did her work relate to specifically?

—I don't know. ¿She was working on a paper?

—¿What about her behavior? ¿Had it changed recently? ¿Anything you wanted to discuss with her but she refused or was evasive?

—No.

—¿Her health?

—Perfect health, always. From the moment she was born, right there, in this very house, her father handled all her medical care.

She looks around in memory, but I keep perfect eye contact. She continues at length how the good doctor had been obsessive (my word) about Angelica's health, even restricting in his will who was authorized to handle her future medical care, in the unlikely event she would need any, and the tests they could and could not run. Yes, that.

I send her to find that will and, if possible, the Angelica monograph or whatever.

She goes, and takes forever. During this forever I'm able to mostly avoid the significant staff and have a research run of the place.

Carlotta has told me the truth as she knows it and the space is full of her thoughts on Angelica and related topics. What it lacks is what the world entire will likely lack hereafter: any sense of the missing's voice.

When Carlotta eventually returns she is armed with nothing, just more prayers.

5th entry: obsolescence

THE ARGUMENT

Some action being preferable to inaction, a plan is initiated. But what about the path from essential to inessential, and is it reversible?

Mauro and I are at an open-air café. Everything's open to the air in Cali, not that there's ever any fucking air to open to. And I'm sticking to my claim that there are none, Mauro! As in zero. Not a single telephone booth left in all of NYC.

"Impossible that this is possible," he says. "The communication, you must have it."

"We must and do, but no more payphones."

Cali has at least one because we are staring right at it. Across the street from us and next to the police station, sometimes you get breaks.

"Uy, look at this one, Riv. Look at the shorts, my God."

—Yes, very impressive. But I'm going to ask you to keep your eyes on the phone booth.

"For supposition!"

—You say of course, but even now you're still looking at her.

"No, no. I'm focus."

I make him repeat the plan and he does so perfectly. Maybe he *is* focus, hell do I know?

A police station is a police station, Colombia or not. Walking to the front desk, I am imagining a corruption and malevolence that's likely indistinguishable from the truth. I imagine deep, blameful loss and an unfeeling universe responding with stony silence. This might be memory.

I start slow. Just checking on a missing person's report. Angelica Alfa-Ochoa. The dude pulls out a binder the size of those old phone books.

The bulk is not due to extensive documentation. I'm realizing each person gets one page. Mysteriously evanesce into invisibility one day and a single sheet of paper will replace you. And eventually no one will read it unless someone like me comes in and asks.

Reported by Carlotta Ochoa five days ago, I add.

I want to ask him to put the book away. That together we can find everyone. If we can only remove the ugly film that is the world from our eyes.

Reported here, at this station.

Yes, I'm sure.

He is not with me. Maybe no one is. Maybe no one is ever *with* anyone else. And we just all feel our way haltingly forward into missing person.

Who I am is something he wants to know so he can write it down.

—¿What in the *puta* hell does my name matter? Angelica Alfa is the name that signifies here. She's my cousin and I would very much like to know what steps have been taken to find her. If you can't answer, it's because nothing's been done. ¡And that makes you murderers! ¿Is that the explanation?

Yelling in a police station is a good way to gather a crowd. I start visually scanning it and registering faces, all while continually upping the ante. So now the American embassy is somehow involved and do they know who her father was? For that matter, do they know who I am?

Before they can correctly answer *no one*, I am being forcibly ejected. These guys are all in militaristic green and quick to violence, so I have to be careful to resist just enough to prove a point but not enough that it converts into something annoying like a fracture.

Ultimately, I declare loudly, to all whom my sound waves might reach, that I am deeply offended by the rampant investigative negligence and that their punishment will be that they will never again see or hear from me. They seem comfortable with that. I storm off in the opposite direction of the phone booth.

In contravention of our plan, Mauro is blatantly watching my every step.

6th entry: a grim prediction

THE ARGUMENT

On second thoughts and what comes before first impressions.

"But how did you know?"

—I didn't *know* know. But you rarely go wrong predicting human frailty.

Mauro and I are in a park with a lake. The park, *Parque de la Babilla*, is named after a damned alligatoroid creature that resides in the lake and is depicted in a man-made stone representation that arrogantly rises out of the water. The two genocidal maniac brothers who are irrelevant now but ran Cali in the eighties and early nineties (the Orejuela brothers) used to live feet from the park in two houses that comprised multiple city blocks. And they are almost certainly responsible for the creature's aberrational presence there the way another mass murderer of the buried past (Escobar) gets credit for the Medellín hippos.

"Because it happen just like you say. You should to seen me. I pretended to be eating my *arepa* and got right up to the phone like you instruct."

—¿What do you mean, you pretended to eat an *arepa*? ¿How do you do that?

"No, I ate it. But I pretend that is *all* I am doing, you see?"

—I do.

"Look, I took a picture of the name of the cop."

—That was a needless risk, I just asked you to remember his name.

"Yes, *pero* I got his face too, this way's better!"

—¿But you kept recording from the view we had at the café, right?

—¡Por supuesto!

—Great, send it to me with the picture.

"Send you the, how you say, *surveillance*?"

—Please.

"Transmissioned," he says, and my phone pings.

—¿More importantly, where's your friend? He's late and I'm spent.

"Late? This is Cali, if he appears anytime in the next half hour, that's considered early."

—I forgot.

"You do look rendered."

—Thank you. ¿And he's going to deliver when he finally arrives?

"He's high up with the phone company."

—Nice to know, but that's not my question.

"He will delivery, sure. The phone number the police call from the phone booth after you left."

—¿More than that, right? ¿The name it attaches to and, if a landline, the address?

"Yes, if you pay, for supposition."

"Of course."

"Of course you pay."

An eternity passes before Mauro answers his phone then informs me that his friend is claiming success but refuses to pierce the digital realm in any way to prove it. Also, this informant is running late even by his own definition. I give Mauro an envelope.

—Pay him with that if what he says is true. I'll come by tomorrow at dawn to get the information.

"Where are you going? Is only eleven thirty."

—I can't do another Cali night, man. I need sleep bad.

"*Pero* come early, I have to work tomorrow."

—¿What do you even do?

"I work for a plastic surgeon, here that's like being a priest. Y *este tipo*, man. An office in Miami and one here. The number of patients? You would think is free!"

—¿And what do you specifically do, the surgeries?

"Ha, ha! No, I bring in the patients, *mijo*. I know everyone in this city."

—That I can definitely believe. I'll come super early and text you when I'm outside so I don't disturb Claudia and the kids.

"Ready."

—Good.

"Wow."

—¿What's wrong? ¿Mauro?

"*Mal aguero*, man."

—¿What does that mean?

"Is mean . . ."

—No, I know what it means. ¿But why are you feeling it? The bad omen.

"It's just . . . when that guy come out and walk right to the phone like you predicted. I knew I had to get close like you said and I did, but . . ."

He turns to look right at me.

—¿What?

"I felt, like, *danger*, you know?"

—That's all right.

"You ever feel that? Danger like that?"

—Listen, don't get offended here, but anytime I've ever been in Cali I sense at least a constant low-level menace.

"True, *pero* I live here and I felt it. That's serious, no?"

—Maybe. But, look, just get me this info and we're good. I don't mean to rope anyone else into this.

"So you agree it's a serious rope?"

—She's probably on a romantic getaway —I lie. —I'll find her and get her to call her mom, easy money.

"I don't think so. Remember Nelson?"

—¿Remember him? ¿Kind of question?

"He was so much older, more like father than a brother. I was only fifteen, but as soon as they said he's sick. And they tried to make minimal, you know? Soon as they said he was sick I knew. And less than a year."

—That . . . I don't.

"You were fifteen when your father, right?"

—No, I turned fifteen a few days later.

"Our family, man. You know about our grandfather, shot like that in a plaza. Your father, a child, having to watch him die right there before his eyes."

—Well, ¿who takes a ten-year-old to a Colombian political demonstration?

"It's us, no?"

—Okay, every family has their . . .

"When I got close to that guy outside the police station? It all come up, that past. I felt the part that's true of all of that. Even though those things are different, ¿entiendes?"

—Very different. Terminal illnesses and random violence. The violence, by the way, in 1948. This stuff is ancient history by now.

"And the feeling in my chest?

—Let's stick with facts for now, not premonitions.

"Drop the case, *primo*. I feel it. In the bloodstream."

—Christ, Mauro.

"I'll tell Carlotta you found nothing, that Angelica's almost for sure dead."

—I don't think she is.

"Who cares? Is not your business!"

—It literally is.

"I won't give you the phone information unless you drop the case."

—If I dropped the case I wouldn't need it, but I won't consider dropping until you give me the information.

"And I won't . . . wait, ¿que?"

—I don't know, see you tomorrow.

"I think this is a very bad thing that's happening. I think there's another world that's on the side of this one. If you're on this side then you're lucky and blessed and you don't go to the other. You don't go there on purpose. You just pray you are never pulled into it. You're talking about going there without force. You're not being forced to go, you want to go! You been better off not even coming here if this is why you came. Why did you come? I'm responsible, I connect you with Doña Carlotta, now what? The other side, why? Tell me you will to abandon all this. I'm responsible."

—Easy, man. It's not all you're making it out to be.

"It's worser, I was being optimism!"

And as we wallow in that, the sound of disturbed water. Then a horizontal V of teeth is emerging from the lake and moving toward us as if the earth itself were expelling an infant dragon through its watery birth canal. Mauro notices but just concedes that the lake and the park belong to this creature. Easy enough when it's not you being stared at by primordial eyes. I take Mauro by the shoulder and we leave the park for the adjoining sidewalk.

I need this day to end. Events just keep coming. I guess that's always true but usually they don't stay long in order to make room for the new ones. These events are persisting until they crowd each other impossibly.

But even then it's not really *worser* like Mauro claimed. It's neither worse nor better.

It is, more than anything, the Present.

7th entry: the vast unremembered

THE ARGUMENT

The relationship between the incidental and the
momentous exists outside the scope of recollection.

Only thing this present is good for is distracting from the past. But something that relentless can only ever be quieted, never erased. The past part that keeps coming back to me now shouldn't even be particularly memorable.

Not long after Jane moved in, so maybe two years ago, there emerged the need for a lampshade. And through the silent and invisible relationship machinations that often proliferate, the task fell squarely on Jane. While she attended to that, I busied myself with the kind of empty domestic gestures that serve mainly to distract the mind. Empty except that one of them resulted in the irreparable destruction of the very lamp at issue.

About this lamp. To the eye there was nothing distinctive about it. But to Jane it had resonances. One of those objects with the ability to involuntarily transport a person through time. Jane said it wasn't so much a question of remembering the lamp as it was an inability to remember a time before the lamp, and what that does to the mind involved. And Jane very rarely spoke of her past, so that imbued the whole thing with a special, as in limited, potency for me.

At least until I destroyed all that. I remember I tried to contact her so she could abandon her pursuit as suddenly unnecessary. But getting Jane to accept a communication was always a fifty-fifty proposition at best and this one dissolved unanswered into the ether.

Next thing was her in the doorway, palpably pleased with her purchase, though I confess to detecting nothing extraordinary about it.

The next moment was like I had lost the power of speech as I silently gestured toward the wreckage. Jane also avoided words. Instead she slid onto her knees, that's what I most remember, and began to sift through the remains of the lamp like a jaded archaeologist. When she stood up, it was as if an unseen force had initiated her rise.

"It's just a lamp. After all. A lamp."

"Sorry?"

"It was here and now it isn't. And you'll say where's the receipt? That if I had kept it I could return the shade."

"You don't need a receipt. I'll get them to take it back."

"Let's say you do, will that bring the lamp back? What about the light, everything now in the dark, the light. Ever think how much of human history was spent just making it so we can see in the dark?"

"No, but it's a brilliant thought."

"Hmm."

"Get it?"

"Not now."

"You're right, sorry."

"Oh, no! Not that kind of thing really. Probably just being dramatic for the fun of it. The world comes at us how it wishes and we must accept it in that form if at all. I'm not actually upset anymore."

It kind of ended there, but this brief Jane performance stayed with me. It was multilayered, true, but also disturbing in its failure to convince. Hard to pinpoint exactly, but it wasn't that I was unconvinced she had emotionally accepted the loss. It was worse than that. What struck me then was how the whole thing combined to create an intimately weird effect. See, I didn't conclude that Jane was not upset about the lamp anymore. But I also didn't believe that she was still upset but pretending otherwise to abate my guilt. It was stranger than both those options. I had a nagging feeling that grew into a belief that the truth was she had never been upset at all but intuited that such an absence would be inappropriate so essentially performed what she thought that kind of upset looks like. Then, because that causes tension, shifted into pretending that she was pretending to no longer be upset out of politeness. Which meant that at the end of it all she was telling the truth while pretending to lie.

Jane was like that.

What is a person? It can't just be the body they occupy, which can change drastically without any resulting controversy over identity. If it's what we call personality, then what is personality? If personality is a kind of involuntary unconscious performance, there still has to be an underlying consistency that creates predictability, not necessarily in actions but at least in the actor.

With Jane, she was just never going to give you that consistency. Too often it felt like someone had been given the relevant facts and was doing an impersonation of Jane, and now the world would have to learn this new Jane. Then she would switch back as if all that never happened and you had merely imagined it. And even though you grew to realize how enervating it could be to not have that kind of consistency, any anger wasn't really going to land on her because, above all, you knew no one wanted that consistency more, and would have benefited from it more, than Jane herself.

When Jane left she took all that with her, replacing herself with an explanatory letter but cruelly leaving behind my thoughts on it all.

8th entry: the view from here

THE ARGUMENT

*Stare at something long enough and you can see through
to its pneuma.*

The hotel is haunted. This is fact, not opinion.

The tall suit with the intimidating woman inside is explaining
this to me. Not because I've betrayed any interest in the topic, just
to kill time while her coworkers cowork to rectify the problem.
The problem is that I am in almost tearful need of my bed, their
bed, and the access key that worked fine this morning won't work
now when the stakes are much higher.

The spirits grant or deny access at their discretion, she says.
I've probably heard how Colombia is known for its haunted ho-
tels. Everyone wants to talk about the Santa Clara in Cartagena.
A former seventeenth-century monastery. And it is beautiful and
it is haunted. But the spirit world has no less of a geography than
our own, do I understand?

I tell her I do so she'll stop, but instead it functions as a kind
of invitation.

—¿For example, you're American, yes? ¿Are the States and
Colombia the same? Surely you see the profound differences.
¿Why do people think the spiritual world functions otherwise?
¿Tell me, would you rather live in a Bolivian penitentiary or in a

Tuscan village? This place has been here, in some form, for all of the city's almost five hundred years. Imagine the events that have occurred here, this very spot we now stand on, you can feel it if you try. This is no pearl of beauty in Tuscany.

—Looks fine.

—¿And what do you tell me of people, are all people the same? ¿No one would say they are, but what happens when we picture phantasms? We always stupidly project uniformity when we picture the unknown, like when space invaders or people from the future all dress and look alike. The story here is worse even than allowed by human imagination, the same we just said is so weak it can't even conceive how the world of spirits is as rich and varied as our own. Now imagine the kind of ghosts the slave trade produced. You're thinking of the victims, and in the case of Cartagena, *the* major Colombian slave port, you would be right. ¿But you know who lived here, where we now stand? The same devils who've always lived in Cali: the architects of Pandemonium.

—Okay.

—¿You know about Pandemonium? Then you know that when God defeated and cast out the rebellious Satan, he and his minions of fallen angels had to regroup and plan their next move. Coming to in hell, *Satanás* called for the formation of a council. This demonic council would advise on the best course of action, so long as it was steeped in vengeance. The resulting debate was held in Pandemonium, the newly created palace and capital of hell. Less known is the fact that the response they decided on, perverting human affairs at every turn, required an earthly base of operations.

Just then, blessedly, a new key card arrives. Now she's simultaneously letting me in and telling me I should check out the next morning.

—¿Do you understand what I've been explaining? —she wonders.

—I don't believe in haunted places. Or the spirits who would do it.

—¿Truth?

—Truth. Places are just that.

—¿Do you have a childhood home?

—¿A what?

—Where you grew up.

—Yes.

—¿If I told you today it was going to be destroyed tomorrow for firewood, would you want to see it one last time? You would, because places and locations have spirits, no different than you.

—The hotel is haunted, you're saying.

—More than that.

—The hotel is Pandemonium on earth.

—No.

—¿The hotel's not haunted?

—It is, but only because of where it is.

—I see, Cali's haunted.

—No, ¡the entire valley! ¿Can't you tell?

—¿That the entire valley is haunted or infernal? No. This is one of the most naturally beautiful places on earth, explain that.

—Nothing to explain if you're familiar with the ways of Satan. And you only see beauty because you're unaware of everything that's happened here. Especially the rivers. ¿Should I put you down for checkout tomorrow morning?

—Boy, the owners must love you.

—I am the owner.

I wake up as if into a conspiracy and right away know it's wrong. Too early and too awake with no alcohol or noise to distract.

Making everything worse is that I fell asleep with the Mauro video on the giant TV screen and with it frozen on a close-up of the corrupt cop at the pay phone.

I can't find how to turn it off, so I just end up staring at that face until it feels totemic. Is there any way I know this person? Because the face is familiar.

Then the spell breaks and I reflect on how little I know.

Maybe Mauro's phone company connect will come through.

Because something happened. Something.

And how often that's the only thing I'm sure of. I may not ever be able to identify or explain what that something *is* precisely. But I will be able to confirm to Carlotta, and anyone else who cares, that she didn't imagine it all.

She was born into this world, Carlotta. No one can explain why. And if she was the sort who never thought deeply, or did but the result was a détente of tolerance with meaninglessness, that was only until now, when forced to face the aggressive nullity of not Death but something worse.

A sudden disappearance is worse than mere loss, the greater harm intellectual and therefore spiritual in nature. Where once she murmured anonymously, spectral Angelica now has the potency of an infinite sun.

And here I am, tasked with defeating all that in a place the hotel owner claims is the seat of human evil. And I can't turn off the screen and I am alone without noise and, but for that face, it is otherwise perfectly dark.

Including me, I am dark, still spellbound by the face and in particular its eyes. Eyes that I've decided are the element I've seen before.

Black eyes in a strange shape.

I need to sleep. To forget then remember instead of always presently sensing. Because of the eyes I'm not thinking, autonomic responses only.

I force myself to think, not just see or feel, about those black orbs. They are hate, toxicity, avarice, deceit, and I suddenly know where I've seen them before so that finally I can rest.

The caiman that skulked out of that lake before.

That creature had the same eyes.

9th entry: the indivisible invisible

THE ARGUMENT

The universe of possibility constricts at least a bit.

Where I am is under a giant cat. The cat is eleven feet tall, weighs three tons, and is pointedly not looking down at me as I sit dumbly at its feet. It just stares out sightlessly.

I'm too tired to read thoroughly, but it seems I should care about sculptor Hernando Tejada. The bronze creature, *El Gato del Río*, is his creation, and when the creator died there emerged a clowder of much smaller descendants forged in the creature's general image. These sculpted beasts then gathered near the Cali River in the north to form *Parque el Gato de Tejada*. And I don't like being in places named after people, but this is the park I currently sit in at Mauro's cloak-and-dagger direction.

The promise is information. Mauro's guy has come through with who got that call from the precinct. Mauro doesn't want to discuss over the phone. Meet him at the cats, he says.

When I first spot him, he's looking at everywhere and everything but me. And all jumpy. He finally arrives but won't sit.

—¿Your friend came through for us?

"Yes, for supposition he did."

—¿With an address?

"The worse kind."

—¿What does that mean?

"See for yourself," and he hands me a paper:

Elenia Mondragon
Avenida de las Américas #33
Norte – 26

I read it and look up.

"So you see what I mean," he says.

—Not at all.

"Mondragon. *Mondragon!*"

—Okay.

"Mondragon."

—I heard you. Three times now. ¿What does it mean?

"Is mean it's over. We're in big under our heads."

"Over."

"Yes, it's over."

"No, *over* our heads, not under."

"Exactly. We're going to lose our heads!"

—Let's do this. Tell me, *in Spanish please*, the reason for this terror.

—The terror is Mondragon, that name.

—Okay.

—That name owns this city.

—Don't fuck around, Mauro.

—You have a point there. He owns a side of this city. The side that malfunctions and the malformations that result. Everything dark that spreads in opposition to light and life is darkened by it. Every bloodletting here is Mondragon. Exeter Mondragon in particular.

—Never heard of him.

—That's the genius of the man. Unless you know where to look, he's a specter.

—¿What about that address?

—That address is exactly what I'm talking about. That's basically *Torre de Cali*. The tallest building in the city and Mondragon through and through.

—But it's not exactly the tower.

—Correct, a private home across from it.

—One registered in that very same, you say infamous, name.

—Of course, hiding in plain sight, the most dangerous kind of hiding.

—¿So what does it mean that the cop's call went there?

—It means there's no chance anymore of an innocent explanation. No possibility of a happy ending here. A girl disappears without a peep. And when a private detective goes to the police to press the investigation, an officer skulks out and calls Mondragon. ¡Mondragon! His boss. His boss because Mondragon owns the police. That's it, there's no way this is anything but tragic. This is a closed case now.

—¿Closed how exactly? We don't know anything.

—We know every single thing I've just said and that's enough. We also know Angelica's dead. You were hired by Carlotta to bring her daughter back and now there's no one in the universe who fits that description. A case is over when you have either failed or succeeded and you have failed.

—I haven't failed.

—¡You can't succeed, same thing! You can't resurrect someone from the dead. You tell Carlotta tomorrow that Mondragon is involved and she'll understand that it's better to let things drop rather than add more bodies to this nightmare.

—First of all, I wasn't hired to bring her back. I was hired to find out what happened. And regardless of her status, I have not done that. Second, I'm not so sure she's dead.

—Come on.

—Hear me out. ¿What do you think is the extent of Angelica's involvement in the Mondragon world?

—Poor beauty. She's a cube of ice that just got dropped into the wrong drink, probably thought she could keep from melting. But God knows it doesn't take much with those people. That's why our involvement ends here.

—I don't think so.

—¡It has to!

—I don't think her contact was minor. Think about it. You say Mondragon owns the police.

—Because he does.

—¿But that doesn't mean they're instructed to call him every time they issue a parking ticket, right? No, this was momentous enough to warrant an immediate call the second I left the station. And to someone high up enough to be essentially at the tower. Judging from that reaction, I bet she's alive. Corpses don't generate that kind of urgency.

Mauro wants to know what it all means. If I'm so convinced she's alive, and I'm not willing to close the case, what then? I tell him I have a plan but that to speak it aloud at this moment would deprive it of its power.

We've been walking, but so slow we're only about halfway through the cats. We take the loop and head back toward the giant one. The river is on my right.

When I point to it down there, Mauro shrugs. I don't accept this answer and he says it has to do with Venezuela. People, families, leaving there in haste, for obvious reasons, on their way to Ecuador.

When I counter that what I'm looking at looks more like a village, he says yes, a village of people leaving Venezuela for Ecuador. This only creates more questions in and from me. Like why Ecuador and not Colombia, and how the last thing I sense when I look down at them is movement. There are no answers.

Because these people are *in* the river now. Washing clothes and pots. Children splashing each other, bent adults with sunken eyes.

While slightly above and all around them, a kinetic city. Traffic noise and smells. Commerce and fashion choices.

Below that a mother is unwrapping something. A semicircle audience forms at her waist. Their reaction to what emerges is like no reaction at all, but each knows to take one bite at a time as the fragile object arcs from one congregant to the next, then back again until vanishing. If asked whether the object truly ever existed, I couldn't swear to an answer.

We're at the last small cat, then back where we started. I ask Mauro if he saw it. If he saw what just happened on the banks of the Cali River more than a fifth of our way through the twenty-first century.

He says it's commonplace. But did he see it? He says he both saw it and didn't see it. And that the only reason he even partially saw any of it was through me, because I was with him.

Now it's his turn to do the asking. Am I going to take his expert advice and abandon this Angelica business before I end up dead?

Tejada's cat, her unfeeling stare remains fixed. Traceable, ultimately, to the final horizon. That blur where Earth and Sky call a truce.

I say no. That I won't be abandoning anything. That I am going to do my job. Every step of it. Whatever that means here.

And if I end up dead as a result? Well, then, at least I won't have to live anymore.

10th entry: reflection versus refraction

THE ARGUMENT

The mental life and its limited real-world utility.

I didn't really have a plan when I suggested to Mauro I did by saying I had a plan.

But I do have an address. So after parting from Mauro at the park, that's where I head. And everywhere I pass along the way comes a flood of acetylcholine. Because I then remember or maybe realize that my mother's side of the family, so not Mauro and them, were from this area (northern Cali's Santa Monica).

When I was eight I spent a summer at my grandparents' house there. I remember missing English but not much else.

Supervision was at best lax. Like when we gathered to shoot off fireworks and I heard say that one of the girls present had previously lost an eye to the practice. I wondered if a glass eye could see.

Another time I watched two sickly longhaired men engage in a protracted but ultimately fruitless quasi-swordfight, but using long sticks supplied by the street.

One of them had walked by the house same time every day wearing a ragged army green jacket, so I was rooting for him during the eventual draw. My grandmother dismissed the battle as inconsequential because it featured two *marijuaneros* and scoffed at my suggestion that my grandfather give ours a job at his garage to spur his rehabilitation.

These were events I *saw*. Events that, because of my incidental receptivity and other weaknesses, then seared into my memory as durable images somehow more lively in the present than in the past.

But there were also primarily auditory memories that played on my accursed verbal sensitivity. Whispered references to human extremity. Of dead babies sewn up with contraband inside. Of men forced to dive headfirst into empty pools to become paralyzed. Ears cut off on buses to free the earring.

And all that so persisted mentally in me that decades later I walk through Cali with a weird admixture of adult cynicism and childish stupor. I don't know what I hope to accomplish, but I resolve that I will find the house. Maybe I think that if I just occupy that space again, the same person and location but also not, I will experience some version of revelation.

But not really knowing my way, I walk for hours. I have a vague sense that I need to find a nice residential neighborhood at the bottom of a significant hill, but that isn't much to go on. I give up. The place exists solely in my mind.

In that mind, the girl with the glass eye and radical refusal to learn from past experience is real. The two overaged street urchins swinging to embarrassingly quick exhaustion, they exist. Exist independent of any attendant facts.

They are instantly summonable but utterly unreachable. And that last part hits me hard just then.

A universe of connections. But at any given moment multitudes of them severing or just plain expiring.

The expirations were the real blight. So maybe that girl was now a thriving woman. Or maybe she'd ceased existing altogether. Either way, that moment, fireworks being laid out, the grim revelation, the visual of the girl's face, the eight-year-old's silent analysis suffused with horror and pity, all that had a very fragile existence.

It all resided in and depended on me. And I would, maybe soon, cease to be, taking the *not invisible but visible only to one* event with me. Meaning that universes infinite-fold had already been expunged in this manner.

I thought of New York again but for the first time as a place you run away from. New York depended on no one or thing.

The last letter Jane wrote. A suddenly emptying apartment in the city is like an open burial plot awaiting imminent mourners.

She was smart, Jane, to want rid of me. It wasn't about success or failure, it was about the sinking boat we're all on.

What had I accomplished, really? Close to half a century of litigating the trial of life and at best a deadlocked jury to show for it. Smart to get away from that.

I'd come to Cali to forget and now hadn't. Rumination and recollection are for the idle. I had a purpose and the best kind: one with an expiring clock. I shake off all unwanted brainwaves and restart for *Torre de Cali*.

The way is hard. The distance considerable and I'd been walking all day. Exhaustion into pain until I just have to sit. On the sidewalk itself near a dumpster.

After a while I stand up and remove my shirt. I drop into the dumpster then drag it through the garbage, a lot of it wet. Then I put it back on. In that mess is a half-eaten donut. I fish it out and eat it, retching several times so that tears fill my eyes. Then I rip a hole in my pants, cake my hands in nearby dirt, and resume the journey.

By the time I get to the tower, it's all a bit unclear. At first I forget why I am even there. Everything just looks so deeply unfamiliar. No one looks at me and I find myself making sure I look at no one. I feel mostly that I have somehow inappositely slowed into achieving a kind of escape velocity from the world itself.

But then, over time, it all coheres. And soon I am gathering the cardboard and plastic I will need for the night's shelter. I am hungry, and tired. But now that I have reached my specific destination, and set up my pop-up housing, I am loath to abdicate.

I am in the perfect location. I stare. The house that fielded the phone call. Certainly not modest, but not over the top either. Above all, it seems strong, like a fortress. Or am I just imputing what I know?

I make sure nothing entrance- or exit-related can happen at that house without my awareness. I can even see inside the structure through both a bay window and a second floor balcony.

At first nothing happens, to the point that I assume no one is home. Then it gets dark and that special Cali lighting. That electric dim yellow is everywhere and suddenly there is life in the house. I stare intently, trying to interpret what I see and learn what I need.

No Angelica, that would be too easy, but also no subtle signs of her either. No women anywhere, never a good sign. No overt criminality, true. Still, this is also no picture of placid domesticity. The scene is charged by something and I just know, above all, that I have located meaning.

Now it's just a question of vigilance. I am spent, but I understand what needs doing. Both spirit and flesh are willing. I know not the hour of revelation but know it will be that night. If I can just stay alert, the secret to Angelica's disappearance and the path to redemptive triumph will reveal themselves.

But sitting under the cardboard canopy I had created, the blood on my palms forming rivulets through the filth they cradle, I lay my head on a piece of abandoned tire and fall asleep.

11th entry: a watch

THE ARGUMENT

*How the act of observing something necessarily alters
that thing.*

What wakes me is a pulling sensation. My face is being distorted
by universal forces I don't understand. I don't want to open my
eyes to it all. When I do it's only because my face has gravitation-
ally hit the sidewalk from a sudden lack of support.

Standing above me and looking menacing are two rough
rusted pipes of men. One of them is holding my tire pillow.

"The fuck, man?"

—This is our tire now.

"I see, then you won't mind being beaten senseless with it."
I suddenly really don't want to lose that utterly worthless piece
of tire.

They don't understand my words but clearly divine their intent,
at least judging from the way they stand. One of them has something shiny in his hand, but I'm so disoriented it's like I don't care.

I need to get on point and assess the threat level here. But before
I can even make strides toward that, the bigger one is asking me
what's in the bag and is all on about how it will also soon be his.

The bag is full of purposefully accumulated garbage. It has no
value beyond decoration. Also, I have thousands of dollars in my

pocket. The creation of any kind of scene here would invalidate everything I'd hoped to achieve during the purely brutal preceding hours.

I stand up. I say, in Spanish this time, that nothing from inside that bag will ever belong to anyone who isn't me. That they can either return my invaluable tire fragment, with accompanying apology, or receive the beating of their wretched lives.

I think that in the homeless community I'm now a part of, I must cut an impressive figure because they drop the tire and leave.

I collapse back into a seated position, try to get my heart rate back down. But it won't slow. It won't slow and the cigarette I light tastes like animal viscera. I flick it away and look for my bottle. I find it and the couple of splashes of *aguardiente* therein but then I toss that too. It's like seven in the morning, not sure what I was thinking.

The store I need opens at eight. I stare at the house but it produces nothing. That's a night-oriented crowd in there. And because I literally fell asleep on the job, I have accomplished nothing.

Maybe I shouldn't say that. I have a highly relevant location. Everything I'm seeing, even now, is making me confident that I have picked up a relevant scent.

Problem is all the things I don't know. I may be engaging in an empty exercise, for one. Angelica may not be in there. Worse, Angelica may no longer *be*.

Worse but not worst. Because she could also be in several places at once, scattered all over like dirty doll parts in a landfill. Or she might be in one piece but that piece could be begging for death as a better alternative to whatever violent depredations it is currently enduring. And if any of that is true, then the extent of my future role might be nothing more than sacrificing myself at the same altar.

Other questions. How does some privileged MIT coed get mixed up in this whole Mondragon underworld? Is the Mondragon stuff even real? People always want to believe in some overarching order, even if it's nefarious, so long as it's not all just chaotic lightning strikes. But wishing doesn't make it so and, in my experience, criminality owes a far greater debt to chaos than order.

I am in a good spot, a perfect vantage point, and I am invisible. Not literally, but what few people wander nearby look through me and into the distance. I have no presence but for my watching, and that watching soon becomes a deep stare rewarded only by static emptiness.

It's hypnotic, the big zero before my eyes. In my trance, nothing exists but that house near the tower and me. Then even I fail to exist. Just that house as locus for all the world's uncertainty.

I grow to think, or maybe *feel*, that Angelica is definitely in there. That one of the things that's possible in our shared world is that I can take a kind of mental flight into that charged space, connect with the part of Angelica that takes mental flights, and that connection will morph into the clarity of answers.

But obstructing all that, always obstructing and always everything, is the same physical world that locks us into a cage and steals our voices.

12th entry: reciprocity

THE ARGUMENT

To see clearly, first stop looking.

Back at the haunted hotel, the same woman who informed me of its special status is now telling me I've been displaced. Moved to another room. A better one, I'm assured.

Only real difference I sense is the massive unsettling exposure. One of the walls is a full curtainless window that overlooks the city and makes me feel I'm onstage. And not sure whether to strut or fret.

I am, let's say, *curious*, how a hotel can just do this. Then I remember where I am. There's a highly unpersuasive explanation being given for the displacement, but the only part that stands out is when she says she assumed I was dead after days passed without contact. I remind her that I've paid in advance in cash and she exaggeratedly looks me over before commenting that apparently my presumed death wasn't all that far from the truth.

Once she exits, I reinsert myself into the world of ones and zeroes run by our digital overlords to find that Mauro has been there aggressively worrying my absence. I text him confirmation of my continued survival and we agree to meet tomorrow morning to compare discoveries. I'll tell him then that his involvement is over.

For now I just want to think without acting. The physical suffering of the last couple days has soured me on what mystery-solving, if any, a human body can do. And there's plenty here to trouble a mind.

Start with Exeter Mondragon. Mauro was right that if you stayed on the surface, he basically didn't exist. But every surface has to allow penetration below itself. And beneath this surface? Different story.

See, Mauro had sent me all these links he said lived in the darkest web. Those links lead me to a mirror online world every bit as convincing as our primary one; and in it everyone agrees on the necrotic primacy of Exeter Mondragon, with ample stories of his rise but not a one confidently predicting his fall.

The rise was equal parts meteoric and bloody. And repetitive. Time and again, again and again, time after time. Whenever Exeter Mondragon would arrive at a crossroads, a moment where his future dominance could truly be said to be in doubt, people would suddenly disappear. And these disappearances always helped Mondragon's tentacles extend rapaciously.

The legend is that he started at ten, selling counterfeit tickets to bullfights and other events, graduating incrementally from petty to major to global criminal. From abject hunger to likely the richest man in the world, if anyone would ever be allowed the access to count.

But there's a competing narrative as well. In this one, Mondragon is actually a son of insane privilege. He is educated to the extreme and impossibly brilliant, but his restless intellect can only be sated by unprecedented monopoly, in this case monopolizing global criminality through a subterranean network of unfathomable complexity and nuance.

Which of these narratives, if either, is accurate, is more than just irrelevant. It's as if the question is simply inapplicable to this context. About Mondragon, all possible narratives, even competing ones, can be simultaneously true, and true without birthing inconsistency. Because by now Mondragon is as much concept as man and the malleability of the concept of concepts means they can embrace even contradiction if need be. Here, the expansiveness rises almost to the level of omnipotence. It becomes difficult to judge even things like possibility and plausibility using the usual criteria because the base fact of Exeter Mondragon makes you doubt even the criteria used to judge the criteria.

For example, how can he possibly be convincingly identified by some as the most proximate cause of the Banana Massacre, a vile series of events about which libraries have been written but which occurred in 1928?

Sitting there in the dark, reading about this man after nights spent sleeping on the street, I decide it's not about this kind of possibility. It's somehow about human possibility instead. Human possibility, but possibility in both directions. What would I be capable of to avoid going back to the street permanently?

I have to stop. I am tired and weak in a demonic hotel within a hallucinatory city and Exeter Mondragon may as well be in there with me, so great is his sudden omnipresence.

I'm trying to identify what precisely it is that surrounds me so palpably now. Whatever it is disrupts even my breathing. It's anxiety, sure, but also more. It's the secret of the universe that's been revealing itself to me for nearly half a century and is now swallowing me whole. That Mondragon is not an exception, just exceptional. That people like him discern the greatest truth. That the world takes place on a giant rock and everyone in it derives from that same substance. Life as just a giant sifting pan, pebbles in constant collision to avoid falling through to their finality.

13th entry: where troubled waters flow

THE ARGUMENT

The selfsame substance that feeds our world, the very essence of everything physical, is also a powerful concealer of human sin.

The problem with the specific world I'm in now is not just Mondragon but also the rivers.

See, Cali is lousy with rivers, a ludicrous seven major ones run through it like veins coursing through a failing heart. They are perfectly unavoidable. But also endemic is the perversion of their natural essence. Because you think of rivers as bountiful and life-generative, but here is different.

Take the Cauca River, a six-hundred-mile descent into collective madness. So where once its nutritive flow gave rise to cities like Cali, today it's often called the River of Death. Death because the river is full of human bodies. Bodies that started in the nineteen forties with "*La Violencia*," continued through the height of the drug wars, then culminated in the insurmountably vile concept of disposable human beings.

Who invented "*Los Desechables*"? Probably a concept didn't need much inventing. Like everything feral now extant, many point to Mondragon. Others disagree. As with really everything in that sphere, it feels difficult to separate away any truth.

Whatever its origin, the result was the same: social cleansing. Yeah, that fucking atrocity. Prostitutes, addicts, the homeless, impaired children, the usual list in these situations. Where a mythical high-functioning society would struggle with notions like obligation and fairness, the evil don't do struggle. They just round up anyone they can find in these and other categories, violently end their lives, replace their viscera with rocks so they'll sink, somehow inscribe the words *Cali Limpia, Cali Linda* on them, then dump them into the River of Death in such numbers that the cost of dealing with the subsequent washing up of bodies bankrupted some affected municipalities. Take a stick and push the body back toward the center of the river so it will flow downstream. This was common governmental advice.

I decide Mondragon was responsible. I see him everywhere now. Everywhere but in the highly relevant life of Angelica Alfa, disappeared daughter of Carlotta Ochoa.

Try as I might, I just cannot sense the connection. But there has to be one. Like I said to Mauro, I asked about her officially and that immediately triggered a call to the Mondragon world. I reject coincidence here.

That and Angelica is missing, enough said.

Missing as in *involuntary*, as evidenced by the seeming complete lack of communication and pre-disappearance prep work.

Involuntariness, I conclude, means one of two things: revenge or need.

I rule out revenge. Mondragon's fame wasn't built on his concern for proportionality; in his world, revenge necessarily means death. But I don't see that here for Angelica. If she's been killed in response to some wrongdoing, perceived or actual, on her part, then there'd be no cause for the "law enforcement" response we saw. Did they expect no one to ever inquire at all?

Also, what could she have done to offend? Or has the definition of disposable humans expanded to include MIT students who didn't seem to leave the house much? Are they also now just being picked at random to be filled with rocks and dumped in the Cauca?

In my work you can't keep everything in play forever. To progress you stop weighing plausible versus possible versus probable and just decide. So I decide Angelica is alive.

Ruling out revenge and disposability leaves only need. And radio silence since her disappearance means need of something from Angelica herself. Otherwise that ransom note is super untimely. So Mondragon needs Angelica to either do something or refrain from doing something.

He must need her to do something. The dead do nothing, so that's how you get an ironclad commitment to inaction.

Mondragon must need Angelica to do something that he is incapable of doing without her. But he is capable of so much and she . . .

Angelica is, or *was*, what exactly?

Online, she's mainly a series of pictures. These are mostly shot from above and onto pursed lips. But in one of them she's at something called *Bichacue Yath Arte y Naturaleza*. Innocent enough, except that this wildlife preserve has formed a giant and appalling moss creature whose agape mouth serves as her immediate enervating background. It's a still picture, but motion is so heavily implied I can't now unsee it. The natural world sucking in Angelica to swallow her whole. Maybe that's what happened?

But I don't buy it. Primarily because there would be comfort in that. The natural world just operating under its unseen rules; and there cannot possibly be a place in the world that gives Nature greater free rein to explode into such incomprehensible beauty than Cali, Colombia.

No, that's not it. Here, as usual, everything points to unnatural human perversion and its discontents.

Aside from these kinds of empty social media emissions, there isn't much to digital Angelica Alfa-Ochoa. But maybe there's evidentiary value in the handful of official documents Carlotta dropped off. These relate to her daughter's *studies*, as Carlotta called them. So they're full of grandiloquent academese from the Massachusetts Institute of Technology and grandiose plans from their undergrad customer in response.

Seems there was a late-stage change of academic course. So after getting pretty far along as a Mathematics major, there is a request to become a major in something called Computational Biology. MIT seems fine with the overall concept (considerable delay leading to the collection of significantly more tuition) so they formally approve; but they also take the opportunity to remind Angelica that there is no such thing as acquiring one of their Bachelors of Science without you have produced a thesis. And while we're on the topic, please make with your "one-page proposal for your project."

Angelica does so at the last possible minute and reading it now is like when those TV shows stage a laughably-performed reenactment to keep a narrative going.

Student Information
Name: Angelica Alfa-Ochoa
MITID: 300134253
Email: afa2000@studentmail.mit.edu
GPA in Mathematics Major: 4.0
GPA in Humanities Requisites: 2.2
GPA in Computational Biology Major: n/a

Alfa-Ochoa_Proposal.pdf

No Ghosts, Just Machinery

Whatever kills you makes you stronger. Since the dawn of time, man (and woman) has counterfaced the deep questions of depth. The examined life is worth living. A wise man once said this.

In any examination there is the subject being examined and there is the examiner who is examining the examined subject. If an examination always fails consistently for centuries, this begs the question: is it necessarily the subject or is it the examiner? That is the question.

The hard problem of consciousness and qualia, the problem of other minds, the non-identity problem. These are problems. These are the problems that have flummoxed our generations. Flummox no more!

The right tool for the right job. The history of these searches of the intellect is one of an insufficient toolkit taking on a job it has no suit for. We ask consciousness to explain itself, but it can't stop watching the puppet show in the cave long enough to succeed. The problem is one of capacity and the solution is compubiological.

This brings me to my project. Understanding biochemical reaction networks in neural cells is critical to understanding complex biological systems so that our future selves can design high-functioning synthetic biological circuits. Current models are primarily based on one of two approaches. Some make use of a deterministic digital framework that is thought to be largely incompatible with the throughput (nonlinear dynamics, stochastics, high-order feedback, cross talk, loading, resource consumption) characteristic of human biology. Others employ analog circuit design, the century-old art of crafting and analyzing nonlinear, stochastic, coupled differential equations to perform a desired task, often to given speed, precision, input sensitivity, power, load, or part-count constraints and in the presence of noise or device mismatch. Neither approach succeeds fully.

In my thesis, I will explicate a canonical quantum-computing-based analog circuit that maps a wide class of biological circuits, whether at the DNA, RNA, protein, or small-molecule levels, which can be used in order to design schematics that represent their underlying dynamical differential equations exactly. These schematics will one day be applied to humanity's signature biological circuit, creative thought, in a (r)evolutionary methodology.

Key to the scheme is a groundbreaking synthetic microbial operational amplifier with three amplification stages based on DNA, RNA, and protein stages. Its dominant time constant is capable of high open-loop gain and stable, robust, and precise closed-loop performance. This is paired with a synthetic tissue–homeostasis stem-cell circuit with a quantum incoherent feed-forward loop that attenuates negative phase and thus improves robustness and precision of response to routine cell death. Likewise, the use of both asymmetric and symmetric division of stem cells improves feedback-loop performance w.r.t transients and robustness. Data collection will be immaculate.

The aforementioned will have profound implications that implicate profundity. Our pristine data will at last establish conclusively that what we call consciousness or even a mind is purely phenomenological and deterministic. Reducible to neural events that are themselves perfectly predictive through math. The implications will also imply that we can solve for the Granger causality not just for all high-level brain processes but even for abiogenesis considerations remarking on the origin of life as precursor via transfer entropy ultimately to elevated human consciousness and a new inflationary phase.

I don't expect you to understand.

Before I read that again I'm going to need a stimulant.

When I try to leave my room to get coffee, someone from the hotel suddenly appears before me, inches from the doorway. He steps back and says something I don't understand. Except I understand it is not meant to be understandable.

Then he disappears.

14th entry: celestial

THE ARGUMENT

On lenses and mirrors and how there may be no
meaningful distinction between greatly pretending to be
a thing and inadvertently becoming it.

Just as you're not really paranoid if the world truly is out to get you, I'm not really filled with anxious foreboding if this place is truly haunted.

Am I watching or being watched? Not mutually exclusive concepts; I'm convinced I am being watched as I watch.

My homeless stint ended with the purchase of several surveillance cameras that I then trained on the Mondragon house near Cali Tower. Since then I've rarely looked away from their feed on my phone but also never been rewarded by anything out of the ordinary. Worse is the premonition or realization I'm having that I may be involved in a kind of metasurveillance.

I keep thinking of my return to the hotel after placing those cameras. These things only signify after the fact. Am I getting less quick or is that just the way?

Second I return all of a sudden my room is being changed? Imagine a greater act of aggression if you're the Mondragon group than a seeming destitute placing you under surveillance. Surely your preexisting self-surveillance system would be strong enough to capture the act. Hours later I'm in a room that may as well be a naked stage. And what about the guy outside my door last night? No way that guy wasn't up to something with his anemic poker face and flustered gibberish Spanglish.

So I'm under surveillance.

And the weight of that is heavy.

It's a strange thing to be alone yet know you're being watched. You can't just exist; you begin to watch yourself exist.

Course this is more than just watching yourself being watched. This is knowing danger. Because I'm not being watched out of curiosity. This is a prelude to an extermination, like being in the sights of a scope.

I hit upon an idea and decide to go sightseeing. First stop is Jesus, or Christ the King. Atop the Hill of Crystals, watching over all of Cali, is an eighty-five-foot Jesus with his arms outstretched, as if to say *Come at me, bro.*

Cristo Rey is a natural early stop for tourists, so look at me, Mondragon's crew, that's clearly all I am as I get off a hideous bus and start ascending the hill, wearing costume Bermuda shorts and a camera hanging around my neck. I stop to read whenever information is supplied because that's what a tourist would do, but also because I cannot know that words are around and not read them.

The upward trek is itself a work of art. The many ravines I pass through have been purposefully crafted, with telling visuals sculpted into the sandstone and a kind of Christian redemption story its subject.

I linger in the Garden of Eden ravine. What did serpents look like *before* they were cursed to spend their days crawling on their bellies? Did they have legs? These were early questions of mine at St. Anthony of Padua Elementary School in Union City, New Jersey, and they did not go over well.

Arriving at my destination, the physical and metaphorical summit, I find a weird confluence of spirituality and commerce.

The view is heavenly, in a strict sense. All of Cali's rooftops below, above us only Jesus. The commerce is some dude with a camera. Promising he can fit all of the statue in the same frame with all of me. He's got a little portable printer, and when I look at the result his word was true. Still, it's an odd photo. The contortions necessary to fit me with Jesus make for a strong visual dissonance.

And there are other dissonances. The statue is grand and beautiful. There's openness and love. But below is the world.

I perform the role of tourist so well I basically become one. Then I remember that the performance, however skilled, is about nothing more than my personal safety. That there's still a lot that needs to be figured out and even more that needs doing. That empty gazing— up, down, whatever direction—moves and makes nothing. I leave.

On my descent I give short shrift to Eden this time. None of this is about plants and flowers. Even if Jane and I met for the first time three years or so ago at the Brooklyn Botanic Garden, the one time I found myself there almost unintentionally. There was nothing cute about it and nothing happened at first sight. More like two messes consenting to feel less messy for a while.

I was born with an aching heart that beats out of time often. It's doing so now. Which isn't making great sense given how much less exertion is involved going down in place of up. But then my irregularity rarely behaves predictably. There are pills I have for it but I don't take them. I just wait it out when it comes.

This one's bad. And when I stop to try and get my ticker back on time, I realize I'm in Golgotha. The Hill of the Skull. The crucifixion of Jesus. Not sure we needed a precise low point for this humanity business.

Besides, think of a secular gospel of the kind Jefferson and others have posited. It would still be full of all this unmatched wisdom. But then the crime, vilely executing the personification of love, wouldn't even really register in our universe of horrors.

For me, it's the faces will persist. The face on the giant statue is hopeful and open. The face of a world that rewards virtue but only laments its temporary absence. The face on this cross is the death of all that.

Nothing will revive or resurrect in this fallen world and it is so thoroughly *our* world. There's nowhere to go where I won't see that face. But I can't stay where I am.

I need to leave.

I stay.

I stay and watch. Not far in the distance, I can see the other major hill above Cali and its *Cerro de las Tres Cruces*. These three crosses have an even more open and notorious purpose. They were installed as a defense system. Defense was necessary because from its very inception Cali has been firmly ensconced in diabolical crosshairs.

In this case it was the demon *Buziraco* who set his sights on Cali immediately after being driven out of Cartagena. The demon stood on that hill, looked down on the nascent city below, and cursed it to forever propagate evil.

For hundreds of years, the curse gave every indication of being an effective one. So much so that a countermeasure needed to be devised. So in 1837 the accursed came up with the idea that they would ascend that hill with three giant crosses made of *guadua* that they would then drive into the earth to either expel *Buziraco* or at least immure him and his supernatural reach in that limited spot.

It maybe worked? Alternately appearing as the shadow of Satan or as a grotesquely large bat, *Buziraco* seethed in spite. Then, in 1925, a vicious earthquake—did he author it?—razed the three crosses, freeing anew his evil.

Well, it took more than a decade, but in 1938, the crosses were replaced by even larger white ones made of iron and concrete that stand to this day amidst an eyesore forest of commercial and communication antennae. The antennae work, the crosses don't.

I need to leave.

I stay.

15th entry: terrestrial

THE ARGUMENT

We're dying to kill, but violence always has a succession plan.

Cali was established in 1536 by Spanish conquistador Sebastián de Belalcázar. I'm going to say the Indigenous people fought valiantly, mainly because that's how I want to remember them. I want to remember that at some point they realized they wouldn't be overcoming horses and swords and Spanish armor, that everything in their lives, those lives themselves, would be lost. But that still they fought.

Fought but lost. Lost so that Belalcázar could win, create Cali, then die in Cartagena fifteen years later after having been tried and sentenced to death in absentia a year earlier. So, natural causes. Way too good a finale for a prick who, when encountering a place where the men had gone off to war, promptly ordered the slaughter of the women and children.

These are the people we choose to remember, everyone else we forget. I know we remember this particular mass murderer because almost five hundred years later, I am under a statue of him as he leans on his sword and points out to the Pacific.

What is this pointing? I don't care to read the explanation. I decide he's pointing out to the greater world, one that includes the vast future, and laying claim to all that as well. Yes, that's it. No, he's pointing at Torre de Cali and Mondragon. And he'll go on pointing forever, even though the smallest fraction of the country's remaining Indigenous could tear him to pieces and toss him into the sea.

It's insane, the sheer plenitude of people around. Belalcázar probably thinks it's for him but I don't think so. It's this view that draws them. Picnic baskets and cameras. Groups and families and laughter. Unsolicited, an older woman warns me how rampant crime is where I'm standing, which seems verifiably untrue, and adds that I have *victim* written all over me. Maybe I'm a great actor, because I've not often been associated with vulnerability.

The zoo is nearby and I decide that's my next stop because that's what any competent tourist would do.

Afterward I'll stop at the library to pick up some archival material I ordered: the sole surviving issue of the now-defunct *Journal of the Mind and Cerebral Calisthenics*.

I need it because the only other thing I have *in Angelica's hand* is her unsuccessful attempt, at age nineteen, to have them publish her letter to the editor. The dead letter amounts to a critique of the journal's titular use of the concept of minds. According to then-teen Angelica, anyone "properly versed in neural and other networks" would understand that there were no minds. Just a great deal of brains, brains and illusions. The problem of consciousness that everyone was always on about derived from a misguided attempt to analyze the existence of something that lacked existence.

The decision not to publish seemed a good one. The letter occasionally strove for a poetic flourish, but the only effect in me was secondhand embarrassment. Substantively, it seemed to ultimately just boil down to super-strict materialism. And as someone keenly aware at all times of his own consciousness, I've always had a limited valence for these arguments.

Still, her opening had stayed with me and made me curious

about her father. In it she claimed that on matters of science, she was "raised in a heavily monist household." Whatever the hell that means, I know enough to know it must be attributable to her father.

The little I know. Dr. Enrique Alfa was a medical doctor of, like, no renown. He published nothing I could find before dropping dead suddenly about a decade ago when Angelica was twelve. Carlotta had described intense doting that I'd characterized as obsession, but could the obsession have posthumously taken hold both ways so that Angelica now enacted it, even if only subliminally?

Maybe the doctor is the answer to a question I can't yet formulate all that well, but that will have to wait, as I am now paying to enter *Zoológico de Cali*, and watching me intently now is not only a guy I recognize from *Cristo Rey*, but also a fucking lemur.

I think. I'm so bad with animals.

16th entry: orbs neither fully lunar nor solar

THE ARGUMENT

*Only children and artists still believe the moon emits
light, which it does.*

I skip the zoo. Mainly because I'm suddenly filled with the conviction that I'm already in one, but not as visitor, as entertainer. King Lear's Gloucester concludes that the gods treat us the way wanton boys treat flies, pulling their wings off just because. That they kill us as a form of entertainment. A conclusion that maybe forgets how all the mayhem preceding it was pretty clearly man-made. But as wildlife in a zoo, are we. Only I don't believe in a multiplicity. Just a sole watcher. Amused by the staging of our imprisoned behavior and loath to interfere.

I go to Cali's nearby Hall of Records instead. Enrique Alfa published nothing, true, but he lived, he acted. And doing that should leave a mark.

It did, and I compile what I can.

Reading the meager paper legacy Angelica's father left behind, I start to understand. Okay, maybe *understand* is too great a claim. I gain something like pre-knowledge. Of a through line that encompasses Angelica, her father, and Mondragon. Although maybe just the resonances of the overarching one that envelops us all.

Some documentary facts in chronological order, scant but maybe telling. The eventual Dr. Enrique Alfa was born in the home of his mother under the supervision of a first-time midwife (birth certificate) then baptized Catholic two days later (baptismal certificate). Not present for either blessed event was Enrique's father who, it is helpfully explained (*ibid.*), "died during gestation."

Seventeen years later, Enrique is listed as sole surviving offspring of his deceased mother (her death certificate). Later that year he legally changes his surname to Alfa then Enrique Alfa enrolls in la Universidad de los Andes in Bogotá. Eight years later, he has graduated from their medical school and Dr. Enrique Alfa is licensed with the title of Physician and Surgeon (Medical Registration of the Valle del Cauca Governor's Office). Curiously for a supposed surgeon, there is no mention of any affiliation or even attempted affiliation with a hospital or any other conventional employer.

Instead it feels like Medicine as Business. So the next official missive is the incorporation of something called Enrique Alfa Amalgamated Incorporated, along with an unsuccessful attempt to register and classify a hypothetical future medical device called the EB³ID, or the Endothelial Tight Junction Blood Brain Barrier Infiltrator and Disrespecter; which device made no specific claims, grand or otherwise, as to what it might one day do (Reporte № 287 del Instituto Nacional de Vigilancia de Medicamentos y Alimentos) yet claimed to be worth in the potential trillions as roughly comparable to the discovery of the New World. All that peters out two years later with the underwhelming sale and immediate dissolution of the company. Ratification of it all somehow involving a strange symbol that feels familiar but that I cannot quite place.

The rest is the classics: Marriage and Death. He marries Carlotta Ochoa (marriage certificate) then leaves her a widow (death certificate). Between those two events nothing (no mentions of Angelica) and nothing as well since. Maybe it's all nothing.

Either way, I'm headed to see Mauro. He has set up a meeting with my client and a *surprise guest* he admits has nothing to do with the *investigación*. This latter part I have no interest in.

But first I need sustenance, of every kind. The street I'm on in *Ciudad Jardín* reminds me more than anything of Rodeo Drive, and fuck Rodeo, of course. Off to the side is a bakery chain everyone goes to, so no way I'm adding to that.

What I find instead seems highly improvisational. I guess it's a house. In front of it is a little courtyard. Through the iron gate is an arrangement of three plastic tables with chairs and a small hand-painted sign. This is Stella's, I gather, and I feel a sensation long absent. I think it's safety.

I need coffee. But looking around, I need so much more. Stella appears to be a one-woman operation. I can see the oven and it doesn't seem sufficient explanation for the blissful aroma narcotizing the air. And she's hung these fruit-themed lights throughout. In other words, I may very well have stumbled into the premier food establishment in the world.

Sitting there (*cafecito, pan de bono, chorizo*) I'm full-on staring at Stella while pretending I'm not. This subterfuge is especially difficult to convey because there's no one else there. She's so compelling it's painful, but I can't quite put my finger on why.

I feel good sitting there. What are we, what am I, that I can feel this way at this instant?

Well, I don't know about you, but I know what I am. I am a child. Not like a child, just a child.

Stella wants to know if I need anything else. Little does she know how much. There's a sense in which what I most need right now is to sit right there in perpetuity. To never again enter that claustrophobic NYC rectangle with all the charged detritus Jane left behind. Normally, the thought of being perfectly alone produces anxiety but now all I can see in it is the freedom. What happens to me doesn't matter beyond me. Which means that when

I act I'm not weighted down by responsibility to others or even self-preservation, should I ever choose to act again.

She cleans the table nearest me and I see now why Stella's physical appearance has been so compelling. Her eyes are orange, man. I don't know if that's even a thing but there's no other way I can say it. And there's this as well. When she serenely closes her eyes I see that her lids are somehow white, shocking lumens that clash with her tawny rest.

So she mirrors the natural world, this magnetic being. Life-sustaining fire during the day then, when light has run its course, its echoes left to persist on inert canvases. The way what gets called moonlight is really just reflection.

How strange, though in the best way. She will never truly see herself displaying this globally rare attribute. But there's honesty in that too. Because the one thing we never clearly see, any of us, is the thing doing the seeing. Tunnel vision, mandated by an impermeable one-way tunnel.

Also anyway, if I'm a child it's only because I'm a child of God. And if that's not an option anymore, then I'm still a child of the universe. *Universe* being one of those charged words that can never be discovered to lack an actual and tangible referent. Referring as it does to merely everything that exists. So there has to be a universe.

And just now it seems lacking in sense to wonder if God is one of those things that exists. It feels more revelatory instead to discover that *God* is neither superior to nor encompassed by *universe* but that it's two ways of saying the same thing. Odd also that this insight is spurred not by something like sitting in the desert under some influence while staring at the pointillist sky, but rather by this.

Because this is miraculous, but only in the way of our shared everyday miracle. That this courtyard I sit in is more than thirteen billion years in the making. All that time, all those elements, to create this unexpected oasis of peace as prelude to what feels like imminent mayhem.

Only I don't think this is some kind of culmination. The whole thing will just keep spinning, merging, and dividing. A perpetual motion machine without volition or deliberation. One that will grind on not only long after we're gone, but in a way that erases the fact we were ever here.

17th entry: entropy and the soul

THE ARGUMENT

*Everything is most like water at the precise moment you
try to squeeze it tight into your grasp.*

I see Mauro and there's that charge when you make eye contact
with someone whose presence you enjoy but have recently been
deprived of. I try to pinpoint the first time ever I saw this face. If
not that, then at least my earliest memory of it. I think I was eight
and he was four.

Mauro remains a baby. He was the baby then, with an eldest
sister and four older brothers, and that kind of conception sticks.

Back then we'd meet in the city, in an area so central it was
literally called *El Centro*. But pretty soon thereafter Fabio del
Rio, his father and my uncle, a retired chemist with one of those
old-school pensions you could live off, in a nice bit of forward
thinking, dropped city living and snatched a nice-sized plot in
La Buitrera, a naturally dense and back then scarcely populated
rainforest-to-jungle area with a river running through it that was
somehow subject to even less scrutiny than Cali at large. Only
seven kilometers away from the city but enough to create a paral-
lax view. And smack dab in the middle of that plot he constructed
an A-frame chalet with a shocking blue roof to break up the otherwise overwhelming green.

I say Fabio thought forward there because while no one was thinking this at the time, today, about forty years later, *La Buitrera* is quite the trendy travel getaway hotspot, as Americans and Europeans tentatively dip their feet and money in, wondering if they might safely partake of its otherworldly natural splendor. The untold secret is that, truthfully, the place is fundamentally not all that different from when it was a favored location for clandestine military exercises and paramilitary reaction.

Mauro is driving me through the winding choppy roads that lead to the structure and I am reflecting on how certain segments of the natural world can function as a record of the past's people every bit the equal of the ones I'd pulled on Angelica's father. I'm also remembering that while I've been recalling it as one central structure, it's actually a series of homes. Because while the chalet remained the centerpiece, as my cousins aged and produced they would add their own homes and families to the land until they so monopolized the area that an outgoing social aggressor like Mauricio del Rio could be almost like the mayor of a kind of del Rio Village.

And now my mind can realize this little makeshift village with photographic force.

But as we pull into the long driveway I see that the only place that village still exists is in my memory, and I suppose in the memory of anyone else who cared deeply enough to keep it in theirs.

Main thing the Present is good at is giving you undeniable reality. Here that means the chalet's roof is almost pure rust with only archaeological evidence of its blue past. There's a wall missing in fact. Exposed as a result is the further fact that one of the *interior* walls is actually a mural. And a striking one at that.

Of course there's a missing wall. That's the constant bias of nature. Left undisturbed, every brick wall will turn into a pile of bricks. But nature will never assemble your pile of bricks into a wall. For that you need a miracle.

Mauro is explaining it all but I'm registering only the common generalities. How older people need proximity to their doctors and how that means the city. About tenants who just stop paying at all, through no fault of their own, then just disappear. And good luck finding a fair buyer.

The particulars don't matter anyway. Here's what does signify. Fabio del Rio created something genuine, yes, but was it built to last? No more than Fabio himself. Who just gradually got older and older until he was basically imprisoned in his own body then suddenly got no older.

Nor is he the only one. Like so many unattended brick walls, our list of people lost to the accretion of time did what all such lists do, swell with members.

To my obvious question of why we are there specifically, a question I regret the millisecond it leaves my mouth, as potentially dismissive-seeming of things like sentimentality, which I know he prizes, Mauro gets all conspiratorial in tone.

—This is the only place he'd agree to the exchange —he whispers. And I know it's serious because we're strictly in Spanish now, as if his precision were nothing to be trifled with in this matter of life and death.

—¿Who are we talking about?

—Beto.

—¿What's a beto?

—Beto. I told you, head of security at *La Torre*.

—¿And?

—You said you wanted surveillance footage of what the Mondragon house on *Avenida de las Américas* looked like at the moment they got the call from the precinct. You know, when you made that big scene at the precinct over Angelica.

—¿And you have it?

"No yet. *Pero* come here *aquí.*" And together we walk to a dilapidated mailbox where Mauro pulls out a discolored yellow envelope and holds it up next to his grin.

—¿Where's the exchange part of this? Because we are definitely alone.

"*Mucho* cloak and dagger, baby. I left the cash here earlier and is gone, see?"

"Yes, why?"

"Because he don't give it for free, have to buy."

—¿No, why this way? ¿Why in *La Buitrera* and not out in the open or even email? Never mind, I know what you're going to say.

—Of course, fear. He's taking a huge chance giving us this. It took a lot of convincing, and by that I mean money.

—Well, let's see if it was worth it.

Because nothing's ever worth anything. Except maybe this time.

Sitting together on a pile of desiccated firewood, staring at Mauro's screen, the footage seems immediately energized with meaning. We've synced it up to the exact moment we know the cop called from that payphone, so what I'm seeing is confirmation mixed with equal parts revelation.

We watch it again, and when it's over I say nothing. I want to know what this slice of the outside world looks like to someone not me.

—Oh, man, Riv. We need our money back, I'm so sorry.

—¿Really? ¿Did you want Beto to stage something for you?

—No. ¡But we paid for a lead!

—First of all, we did no such thing. I paid, or more accurately, Carlotta paid, for surveillance footage, which your friend provided and which appears to be money well spent.

—¿How so, well spent? There's nothing there.

—Play it again, Mauro. From the beginning.

The footage is super clean too.

—Stop it there —and he does. —Look closely at this guy right here going in. ¿Yellow shirt and mustache, right?

—Yes.

—Okay, go.

Just then I get the weirdest sensation that Mauro and I are the video footage and the images on the screen the developing world.

—Look at the timestamp, Mauro. ¿The call from the cop just came in, right?

—Yup, and here walks out a guy from the address receiving the call while holding a cellphone.

—¿Not a cell, right? That's a cordless landline phone.

—¿Says who?

—Stop, look at it. ¿Look at the size and shape of it, you blind?

—You're right.

—Now stare at his chin.

—¿His chin? ¿What?

—Stop talking and stare, it's subtle as hell.

—Don't see anything.

—¡Right there! ¿What's that?

—He turned his head, he's looking at something.

—Keep watching.

—¿Something drew his attention, a noise?

—Uh-uh, no noise. ¿What's he doing now?

—¿Still looking, what's your point?

—¿What's he looking at?

—Can't tell.

—¿You sure?

—That house, there, the green roof.

—¿Agree, but looking or staring?

—Staring.

—Agree again.

—¿So?

—So if I say to you *where'd you hide x?* I bet the first thing you do without thinking is look at where you hid x.

—Maybe.

—That shit cop calls there to say someone's asking about Angelica and this brain surgeon immediately comes out to check that the property is still safe. Instinct. Keep playing it.

—I don't know, he went back in the house.

—It's all right. Keep going, I want you to see something else. ¿There, what's that?

—Okay, a guy leaves the house with the green roof, the house the other guy was staring at. Big deal.

—¿Just a guy? Keep looking. Stop. Look.

—Oh.

—¿Right? Yellow shirt.

—Mustache, the guy from before. ¿What does it mean?

—¿Means a lot, right? We watched him enter one relevant house then leave another even more relevant house. What we didn't see, of course.

—Shit.

—Is him leaving leave the first and entering the second. ¿Meaning?

—Tunnel.

—There's a goddamn tunnel between the two houses.

—That's some Mexican work, Riv.

—A girl goes missing. An out-of-his-depth PI riles up a precinct about her so that a nervous cop rushes to a nearby payphone to call the organization that suborns him and that he knows is responsible for her disappearance. Some low-level henchman gets the call and has enough sense to worry. He can't hang up and go check on her where she's being held because he doesn't want to interrupt the flow of information he's getting. So he does the next best thing. He tells his colleague to go check on her personally while he continues to talk to the dirty cop. The person receiving this instruction, yellow shirt guy, does so in the quickest way possible, the nefarious tunnel. In the meantime, the call's recipient stays on the phone but steps outside to eyeball the place Angelica's being held. When yellow shirt guy is satisfied, he exits the

green roof house in the conventional way and returns to the house
that got the call to report his findings.

—Oh my God.

—Don't bring that into this.

—She's alive.

—She was alive.

—¿You think she's dead?

—Don't know what I think. But I know what I know, and I
know she *was* alive. In the events on that tape she is alive. But
that was days ago.

—True.

—And of course today and every day hereafter is what matters.

18th entry: on magic

THE ARGUMENT

The world as a kind of sleight of hand.

The summer I spent in Cali when I was eight was magical. I don't use *magical* here as a kind of superlative. Someone says *oh that meal was magical* when they really mean that it was very enjoyable or highest quality. But when I say that summer was magical I mean that it literally shared qualities with the entity we call Magic. And only surface thinkers think that entity is an unqualified good.

Consider the most innocent-seeming iterations of magic and note that even those feature tropes like the sawing of women in half or the sudden disappearance of people who were only trying to assist or be entertained. Or how about when they take a guy, wrap him in a straitjacket or something, then drop him in a tube of water?

Harmless, you'll say, because of the ultimate result. The reveal, a reembodied woman, a discarded straitjacket, reveals that there are no permanent negative consequences.

The magic is knowing that, in reality, negativity is all there is. Everyone will eventually be disembodied, everyone is trapped, everyone will disappear.

Meaning all magic is actually black magic that we sometimes pretend is innocuous.

And that's what I mean when I say Cali, Colombia, at age eight was magical. Part of it was, yes, being eight; but I don't think all of it was that. A lot of it was Cali having the same viscera as skillfully deployed mirrors or chants and spells.

And, just like with magic, I went back to America and left all consequences in that strange place.

But enough of it stayed in my soul for decades that it effected a kind of recombinant DNA in me. A genetic makeup with these intense markers that still emit measurable electricity. Markers like Fernando "Fercho" del Rio.

Fercho is one of Mauro's older brothers, and when I was eight and he fourteen he may as well have been goddamn Aquaman in my estimation. That reference not chosen at random, as that is precisely who he claimed to be as he taught me to deep dive to the bottom of the river we were camping near. Think of the way the world opens up at that age when you add a new skill that before then seemed almost extra-species. Dive after dive with little diminution in the novelty. My father and Fercho's two older brothers, Nelson and Jhon, half-heartedly looking for us while we scrape at the bottom, trying to uncover the lost city of Atlantis.

We never did unearth it, maybe it was never there, but we did accomplish some other unsettling acts that I can't, in the present, make the greatest sense of. Like freeing privately housed ducks for some reason or shooting and missing at a wild boar (self-defense?) with a gun my father had piecemeal smuggled in from the U.S. then assembled in Colombia so he could replace a gift he'd given his square brother, Fabio, who had promptly lost it then loudly longed for a replacement.

I learned to clean fish with sharpened glass. A woman canoed by with her kids and inexplicably unleashed an extended cascade of vitriol at us for staring, which we were in no way doing until she began yelling. Then, yes, we stared. I'm saying it was weird, all of it.

And through it all Fercho was like some granite superbeing who not only always seemed to know what needed doing but also had no relationship with the kind of fear that keeps things undone. And on my two trips here in my twenties, Fercho was definitely still that guy. Maybe we're all just who we are throughout, *in utero* to interment.

About a year ago he'd called me from the blue, thrilled by some new app that made the call free, probably running through everyone he knew overseas until landing on his *gringo* cousin, Riv. I enjoyed the call quite a bit, and I hate the phone. When he told me he was selling Lycra devices that men should wear to involuntarily straighten their posture, I said that sounded promising, then spent the next several minutes less listening to him and more picturing how much the device must look like a bra.

It also triggered a wave of inquisitiveness in me that had me asking Fercho to recount every job he'd ever had: from male-bra salesman backward to the beginning. He took to the assignment the way fire handles paper.

Partial transcript (from memory and translated
inartfully from the original Spanish) of that phone call
with Fernando del Rio

ME: No, I'm just kidding. But weren't you doing security?

FERCHO: For the cyber, cybersecurity. But that was like three jobs ago. No, we got a virus. Finished us off. It was all political, you have to play the game.

ME: A political virus?

FERCHO: Ha! Sonuvabitch virus, man. We're supposed to keep you from getting them and we got one! Bad for business.

ME: I bet.

FERCHO: But right before this, with the posture, was swimming pools, beautiful swimming pools.

ME: Building swimming pools?

FERCHO: Better! Converting them into saltwater. A great success, and built to last!

But then everyone decided they'd rather swim in fresh water. And you know why? Because fresh water is refreshing. So much so that you know what's the first thing rich people getting out of seawater want to do? Rinse with fresh water!

. . . later, much later

ME: What do you mean, you owned a soccer team?

FERCHO: Okay, let me explain Colombia to you. No,

impossible. Here? Here, the Colombian is obsessed with the soccer.

ME: So everyone owns a team?

FERCHO: No, but every business of real size has a company team. Right? Is this found in the States?

ME: I guess, I know what you mean.

FERCHO: Well, I got to thinking. Why can't I have a team?

ME: What business?

FERCHO: No business. See?

ME: No.

FERCHO: Listen, the one-man firm of Fernando del Rio needed a team out there. So here's what I did. I went around and found the biggest degenerates I could find who nonetheless had one relevant skill. Big fat guys who only stopped eating to drink and smoke. But you know what one skill they had? These were expert footballers. And the best kind because they looked like they'd just been let out of jail. So no one saw it coming when the game would get going and suddenly they would come with the razzle dazzle. These guys would smoke and drink during the game! But winning, always with the winning.

ME: How is this a job? Where's the money?

FERCHO: My son, you think we're playing for the love of the game? Thousands of dollars, American, are on the line every game, but only for the winner. And the winner is us, win after win, never a loss. Pak, pak, pak, gol, gol, gol, whenever we need. I had to get bigger pockets. I'm paying my guys real well and still making out like a bandit. Everybody's getting paid under the graceful ambit of the Lord.

ME: Who's the coach?

FERCHO: I'm the coach, and I don't even like the fútbol! I don't know the first thing, but there I am in a fancy suit on the sideline screaming 3-2-3, 2-2-3, whatever the whores comes into my mind!

I'm the coach, the owner, the general manager. I design the uniforms, I make the flyers, provide the *aguardiente*, the cigars. Transportation, I had to buy one of those ugly minivans. You know what it is to drive one of those in judgmental Cali?

But the main thing I was was a promoter. You should've seen me. Tooling around in that ugly vehicle, going from office to office pretending it's an honor to be given the opportunity to be the first team to beat us. And the money just keeps going up and up, win after win.

Same thing every time. Our opponent starts off laughing but ends up losing to a bunch of drunk, broken-down reprobates wearing orange jerseys with LOS DESEABLES in green and special midsections I had sewn by the team seamstress to account for the primary body shape of my team, which looked like a group of giant pears in shorts.

ME: The team had a seamstress?

FERCHO: *Los Deseables* was the hottest team in the world and I even allowed myself to dream that one day I might own the national team!

ME: That's not something that could ever happen.

FERCHO: Of course not, politics.

ME: No, just reality, and what the *national* in *national team* means.

FERCHO: Then it fell apart. I get a call. We can put up zero but at stake is five times what we're used to! Hoo, son, you know what we said to that. But even then, and this is not after the fact, I swear, I have misgivings. Understand me?

ME: Maybe.

FERCHO: I know my city. When someone throws money around,

even just theoretical future money, violence isn't far behind.

Day of the game. Suddenly everything is cloaked in secrecy. We're to meet in this parking lot at such precise time with no extraneous people. No phones or other technology; we had none of that stuff anyway.

Sitting in that parking lot, even my drunkard players can see it's getting pretty dark. How is this going to work?

Next thing we know we're being herded onto a bus without windows—how is that safe?—and being driven out to distant nowhere.

The team is very quiet the whole ride. *Los Deseables* knows it's over. And I'm not talking about the winning streak, I mean *over* over. Everyone's preparing their souls for eternal rest and pouring *aguardiente* down their gullets to drown the fear.

But then a miracle. I'm staring at what the bus driver is seeing when suddenly, like Shangri-La emerging from the mountains, there it is. Maybe we're not dead meat. Because here is the most beautiful private football field anyone's ever seen. Bright lights, perfect grass, stands, scoreboard!

ME: The hell?

FERCHO: Like I said, money equals danger here. Game starts. My guys are giddy. Twenty minutes earlier they were mentally composing their goodbyes to this cruel world. Now their main worry is staying onside. And that's bad news for our opponent. Because my guys are artists when they barely care, forget about when they're genuinely motivated. And where before the only motivation was money, here there's not only plenty of that, but it's paired with what I'll call the exhilaration of Life as intoxicant interrupting Nothing.

ME: Easy, Plato. Make with the facts, I'm rapt here.

FERCHO: Right? You want to know what happens next, yes?

ME: Yeah, I'm funny that way.

FERCHO: Soon I'll pass you to Jeny. She says I tell the story too much. Anyway, the game. We're in complete control. But I'm noticing an odd thing. Every goal we score, the tension rises. Usually it's the other way around, understand me?

Close games are tense, but if one team starts to pull away, a form of looseness will take hold. But here the opposite is happening. As all suspense for how the game will turn out disappears, the air thickens with anxiety. A strange crowd is forming around the perimeter of the field and they don't exactly feel like football aficionados drawn by the action on the pitch.

First clue that's not what's happening is the machine guns they're holding that go from hanging loosely around their necks to in their hands to almost pointing at the field.

You see, true? We win easily but the postgame is far more interesting. We want to take our winnings and run away but they're all about an immediate rematch. We're being noncommittal and, sure, someday we'll have to schedule that, friend. But it becomes abundantly clear that they are talking about an immediate rematch to take place right then and there. My guys are old, drunk, and beat-up. But it's also obvious that these guys aren't really asking, they're telling.

So as their goalkeeper is being almost dragged away and his replacement conscripted, we *agree* to the rematch. My guys are smart, they're getting the picture. So they have one leg in the game and the other is trying to board the bus home.

Problem is, turns out their goalie was the only factor keeping things relatively competitive. So *Los Deseables* barely pay attention until another win is in the books. And those guns are getting closer.

They want to go double or nothing again. We don't. We want our money. Everyone's looking at me. We're not getting our money. We concede that we'll play the next day and they show us where we'll be sleeping until game time. Yeah, bus is gone. It's like one in the morning.

You get it, right? We are not free to leave. The game the next night is basically hostages versus captors and the hostages win again. Still no bus and no bus the next night when we win again. Understand that we have no clue where we even are!

Finally, I tell the guy who appears to be in charge that my guys can't be playing a real game every day. No problem, we'll play in three days. So we start playing, and winning, every three days instead, while basically living in barracks.

All the while it's clear our opponent would rather dig a mass grave out there in the middle of nowhere than accept defeat. And their team is changing too. Every game they have some new players and each time a *Deseable* is telling me what professional team the guy used to play for. But ringers don't matter when you have the kind of chemistry we were deploying. Take two parts of hydrogen and mix with oxygen, what happens? Everybody gets wet! You understand?

But the whole thing had us like those little mice but cute, those little fur balls that . . . those . . .

ME: Hamsters.

FERCHO: And the way they spin with the, with the . . .

ME: Hamsters on a wheel.

FERCHO: I know what you're thinking. Why not just lose on purpose and get the hell out of there? Here's the problem with that. Every game has been double or nothing from the previous one. By now there is life-changing money on the line! And they won't pay it and we keep playing and winning until the main question becomes whether in the end any of our lives will still be there for the life-changing money to change!

Finally, the decision is made for us. They played a game that was really like an orchestrated assault while the referee mostly looked up at cloud formations, at least when he wasn't giving red to some of our most critical players. Even then they barely beat us.

And after this game there's not even the pretense of hospitality anymore. Just throw us on that bus and don't worry about the money because we're even. Not a peso to our names, weeks away from home, beat-up physically, psychologically damaged.

That was the end of *Los Deseables*. That was the end of so much for me. Isn't that always the way?

We had a player, *El Conejo* because he made rabbits look slow, who really the history of football should not be able to be written without a line or two about him. But it has been and it will continue to be. Because you need luck. Luck drives the world, not effort or talent. Like when I developed the greatest *arepa* recipe ever, but Mauro accidentally sat on the bag of cheese on our way to meet with investors.

You need luck. You know the people who had it because they are known. You don't know *El Conejo* because he had none. I had none either. So in my life, instead, I've had about forty different jobs.

Then he put me on with Jeny who, as I recall, started by apologizing for her husband.

19th entry: a tropical bacchanalia

THE ARGUMENT

Why it's sometimes difficult to tell if one of us humans is laughing or crying.

Why all that comes back to me then is that a rude car pulls up to where Mauro and I stand, meaning the surprise guest Mauro had promised, and I recognize the operator and sole occupant of the car as that very Fernando himself and, man, it's been too long and a lot of emotion rushes in all at once so that I have to kind of bend at the knees to absorb it all.

We hug. Then that thing where you step back to better behold the face, then hug some more.

—I thought you were in Spain, old man.

—I only *was,* not anymore. And there's a business opportunity there that I intend to fully exploit, first chance. ¿But until then, how can I not come back to see my man? ¿How long has it been?

—¿Who knows?

—When did you arrive?

—Not sure.

—¿How long you staying?

—Even less sure.

—¿Do you know *anything?*

—Very little, but I'm eager to learn.

We catch up, lightning fast because it's that kind of thing. The three of us in what's left of the *del Rio Buitrera*. Contemplating all there is and solving none of it.

Like with all at-length reminiscing, there's a long list of the dead and a longer list of the forgotten. Strip away the vicissitudes enough and all that remains are the constants. Mauro, Fercho, myself. In this context, we are the only constants. That and the Present. The present is constantly alive and *live* and Fercho wants to turn our attention to it.

—¿You still with that nice woman? She got on the phone that time. ¿Yane? ¿Jan-eh?

—No.

—Jane, and he doesn't want to talk about it.

—¿*Que*? ¿Jay?

—¡Jane!

—¿Can we change topics?

—¿*Como* Tarzan?

—Yes, just like that.

Mauro is reading his phone.

—¿What is it?

—Our client. Carlotta. She can't make it tonight. Tomorrow morning instead. ¿Yes?

—Yes. But remember, *we* don't have a client.

—¿What's going on with Carlotta?

—Nothing. But her daughter's a different story. ¿You know her daughter?

—Not really. ¿Angelica?

—The very same.

—Strange girl. Beautiful, beautiful but strange.

—¿Strange how?

—¿Right, Mauro?

—No, I know what Mauro thinks, I want your view.

—Well, for one thing she spoke Spanish with a British accent.

When she even spoke. ¿And I think even before she ever set foot
in the States, catch my meaning? ¡And they don't speak that way
in the States anyway! ¿Also, women are emotional, no? ¿But her?
You can't upset her. Although, like I said, I don't know her very
well. Not sure anyone does. Of course Carlotta does. I guess.

—I bet she's upset now —Mauro says. —Worse, she has upset
Mondragon, assuming there's still a she.

—¿Mondragon?

—Yes.

—My God —says Fercho, and like a synchronized set piece the
two immediately make the sign of the cross.

—Okay, children.

—Mauro's right, Riv. You don't mess with Exeter Mondragon,
you don't mess with people who've been in a room with him, you
don't . . .

—I get it.

—That girl's gone. Tell Carlotta tomorrow you did all you can.

—Ah, I see.

—¿Good, you agree?

—That's not going to happen. I have too many questions.
Here's one of them. You just said Mauro is right. ¿But how do
you know Mauro's position on this when you're supposedly just
hearing about it now for the first time?

—Uh.

—Uh.

—You got me. ¡Mauro called me in to save your life!

—Well, you did manage to hold strong for a full twelve minutes.

We are laughing and we can't stop. One of those involuntary
mass hysterias that becomes mostly about itself.

When it abates enough to restore some communication, Fercho grows solemn.

—No, I'm serious. These people, it's not like the States. ¿Did
I ever tell you about the soccer team I owned?

—No, but there's no time now.

—Thank God —says Mauro.

—But if you insist on going forward, Riv, then, yes, I'll be part of the team.

—There's no *team*, and definitely no invitation to join one.

—Oh, I see, ¿you're going to let him in but not me?

—¡He's not in either!

—¿What?

—You can have the same status Mauro has.

—Thank you very much. ¿Now what?

—¿How about a night off from all this?

This now is something in their wheelhouse. I lay out the parameters. I want us to eat a lot of food. But nothing fancy, the kind of fare you start regretting right away. And lots of that species of drink that makes everything go down smoothly. Surrounded only by people we know and like and love and none of us has to lift a finger. And music. And women.

This is Cali, so it happens, just like that. We take over a place, maybe twenty of us, and it's perfect. The perfection is all of it, the people, the place, both the details and the generalities.

I make a willful decision to occupy only the moment I'm inhabiting each second. And every time I do I find I'm not in danger or pain or even thought. Thinking, of course, is the tricky element to avoid. Full of complexity and foreboding, whereas sensation just *is*. Sensation is itself and not *about* another thing the way a thought necessarily is.

This sensational in the literal sense night goes and goes, extending out into the world like starlight. So much color, in every sense and everywhere. The food, clothes, makeup; the nature that invades where we sit and stand and dance then sit again and think and remember. And the music, like the city arranged these notes in precisely this way for precisely this night.

By the end it's almost three in the morning, we've created our own galaxy, and everyone in it, people we met that night, people we've known forever, is an individual star, but one that is only able to shine as part of a constellation. Most of us can't stand up real well and the collective power of speech on display isn't especially impressive; but we have all seemingly agreed that whatever anyone manages is in contention for funniest thing ever uttered.

Walking out of that blessed place, I can't help it. I think.

It wouldn't be that hard really. A slight adjustment. Maybe imperceptible except at a great distance. Wouldn't take much. More moments like these. Where strong human connections spread like a contagion to fortify everyone involved against the general darkness. Fewer moments like the one that drove me here from NYC.

Change the ratio that way, feed and feed this benevolent accretion, and maybe, in that world, we could stop bumping off each other and defeatedly searching for consolation. Until then, I have an appointment, in a few hours and in this world, with Carlotta Ochoa. Carlotta is stuck in this world as if it were flypaper.

And in this world it's victims, victims far as the soul can see.

20th entry: pride & persuasion

THE ARGUMENT

The hopeless at least avoid a particular kind of suffering.

Carlotta looks simultaneously worse and better. Physically she's aged years in days. But mentally she seems younger, freer. We sit, once again, in her large receiving room. Mauro and Fercho have driven me there but I've instructed them to wait in the car.

—I still feel you were sent by God.

—I wasn't.

—Just for a different purpose. Otherwise, I wouldn't be able to forgive myself for involving an innocent party in this.

—First of all, ¿innocent? Thanks, but no need to make great claims on my behalf.

—So I'm sorry and may God forgive me. But grief steals who we are from us and leaves just extreme desire, desire for the pain to stop. I saw you then as a chance to escape the torture, but I see now that I wasn't thinking of you as your own person, himself entitled to concern.

—¿What is all this? The last thing I'm owed from you is an apology. I should be the one apologizing that I haven't yet walked in here with Angelica on my arm for you.

—*Ay, mijo.*

—Don't cry. I don't pretend it'll be easy, but I believe Angelica is still alive.

—I do too.

—Good.

—I believe we all live on, in a way, after death.

—I meant literally alive.

—Our all-seeing God sees all, including inside souls, and he knows what was inside mine. That I didn't know when I asked you to help.

—¿Why so much past tense, madam? You asked me to help and I agreed to try. That's what we're in the middle of, my trying.

—I know you tried.

—*Am* trying.

—But I also know the forces in this world and their cruel power. The funeral is in three days.

—¿The what?

—I'm hoping you'll come, I know you never actually met her.

—I *will* meet her. ¿Funeral? ¿Do you know something I don't?

—I'm sure I do.

—I mean definitively.

—A mother knows.

—¿What are you going to bury?

—In these instances you can substitute a beloved object.

—¿You have that?

—Her favorite book of poetry.

—¿Which is?

—The collected works of *Colombiana*.

—¿Huh?

—Dorila Antommarchi.

—Ah.

—I put the letter in there too.

—¿The what now?

—The letter, Angelica's letter, the death letter. Her last statement should be in there.

—¿There's a death letter?

—That's what I call it.

—¿And you never thought to mention it? When I was scouring her room. ¡Or when I repeatedly and directly asked you if one existed!

—I didn't know about it until two days ago when I discovered it.

—¿How?

—¿How could I tell you about something I didn't know existed?

—No. ¿How did you discover it, where?

—In my bookcase, never even thought to look there.

—¿Until?

—Until I was looking for a picture to send her school.

—Let me guess, at their request.

—Yes, an alumni letter. And there it was, right next to the photo album the whole time and I never once noticed it.

—Show me.

—¿Show you what?

—The bookcase. And the letter from the school if you still have it.

She walks me over there to a moderate-sized collection of mostly technical treatises and textbooks. I take pictures of the titles. Time was I would have easily just remembered the titles for future reference. But once I started substituting photography for memory, that was the beginning of the end of that ability.

Then she shows me the alumni letter, pulled from a pile of mail. I read it and look at the pile.

—¿You using this Morales funeral home?

—Yes, how'd you know?

—¿And where's the actual Angelica letter?

—There with the funeral director.

—I need it.

—But the funeral.

—Cancel the goddamn funeral.

—No, I need it. It's a basic human need.

—Following death, yes. Not here.

—¿You think it was easy to plan such a thing?

—I understand, but I need that letter. I promise I'll have it back in time.

—It's not relevant.

—You read it. ¿That what ignited the funeral planning?

—Not only that. But now that I know what we're dealing with, my prayers are for your safety and that this will be the end of the bloodshed.

—¿What is it you think we're dealing with?

—I won't say that name out loud.

—¿And what makes you think that name is involved?

—¡Shh!

—¿You had Mauro fill you in while I was gone, didn't you?

—He's a good man.

—Agree.

—And a smart one. You may be smart too, but he's more than that, he's informed. He knows what certain events signify here, you don't seem to.

—What things will mean here is what we make them mean. Call the funeral home, tell them I'm coming by to get the letter.

—I can't hold on to hope anymore, it's too painful.

—Don't hold on to anything you don't want to. But make the phone call, I'll wait.

—¿Who's in charge? ¿The client or the employee?

—Make the call. Humor me, I'll have it back in time if need be. ¿What do you have to lose?

—I've lost everything. Now I just want to rebuild. ¿You're fired, okay? I don't want to be responsible for what's going to happen to you.

—Me either. But rehire me and make the call. You're worried about me, that's sweet. But I don't leave jobs unfinished, pay or no pay. So you would actually be putting me in more danger if you don't make the call.

She picks up the phone.

21st entry: prophecy as tautology

THE ARGUMENT

How any misgiving, if properly investigated, is
empirically sound.

When I get back in the car, Mauro and Fercho have these defeated
looks on their faces.

"Sorry," Mauro says.

"Yes," I say. "It's all very unsatisfying."

—¿What happened? —wonders Fercho.

—Sounds like Doña Carlotta just terminated the investigation.
Can't really blame her, Riv, probably for the best.

—I'm curious what makes it *sound* that way.

—¿What way?

—You say it sounds like the end. But I know that Carlotta did
something like the opposite. She made me promise I would bring
Angelica back. In return she again promised her full cooperation
and resources. Exactly what you'd expect from a woman whose
entire life is in peril. ¿And, yet, you expected something else?

—No, it's just that.

—Yeah, I know. Mondragon and the futility of it all. You in-
fected her with that shit.

—I didn't mean to.

—It's okay, I know your heart. It's your mouth could be better.

Fercho wants in:

—¿What's happening? —he says.

—Fear, fear is what's happening.

—But intelligent fear —says Mauro.

—¿What's that?

—That's fear based on sound evidence. This fear is justified.

—Maybe —I say.

—No, for certain. I have a sixth sense, Riv. Tell him, Fercho.

—He has a sixth sense.

—And it's telling me there's death here, death everywhere. My sixth sense, cousin.

—That's fine, Mauro. I only have five but they're all telling me I'm not going to abandon a client's young daughter to a pack of sadists.

—So . . . ¿the investigation continues?

—It does.

—¿And what about all the death?

"You mean, in the world?"

—Here, in this situation. My premonitions, they don't fail me. The dead. Death permeating everything and everywhere.

"Nonsense." I hand him a slip of paper. "Now take me to that funeral home."

22nd entry: the promise of services rendered

THE ARGUMENT

Or Death as rebuttable presumption.

On the way there, they fire copious questions at me that I wholly ignore. Until one breaks through.

—¿Let me ask you something, yes? ¿Riv?

—Murgh.

—¿If we have so little to worry about, why haven't you, for a single second, taken your eyes off the side mirror?

—¿That's it up there, isn't it, gentlemen?"

—I suppose, but not like I'm some kind of funeral home expert.

—I am, that's it.

—Fercho, how are you an expert in . . . never mind. Listen, slow down. Here's what I need. ¿See the parking lot? Don't get into an accident, but I need you to make a very late and unsafely sharp turn into it at the last possible second. Coming up. Don't get into an accident, but make it good, meaning bad.

I take out my phone and start recording.

—Mauro, ¿subtly drop your head a bit?

Just then the car jerks right, so suddenly it feels like we the occupants will be flying out to the left. But we don't and somehow avoid enough obstacles to stay in one piece and land in a parking spot.

—¡Holy hell!

—¿What was that about? We could've been killed.

—Nicely done, perfect. Add driving to your many skills, Fercho.

—¿But why?

"Oh, why anything instead of nothing? Tell you in a bit, but first this."

I put my phone away and check my appearance.

—¿You know these people, Fercho?

—No, the guy I knew here left.

—You guys wait here. I'm going to go in and pick something up real quick like.

—¿What, though?

—Angelica's note.

—Oh, shit.

—Yeah.

Never liked funeral homes. I know. And turns out Colombia is no better at overcoming their fatal flaw. But the girl at the front might as well be regulating the entrance to a night club for the festive aura she's giving off. At least until she sees me.

—*Buenas* —I say with a smile.

—¿And? —she says without.

—I guess a lot of your customers aren't in position to complain of their treatment.

—¿I repeat, how can I help you?

—Not technically a repetition, but okay. You can help me by connecting me with Morales.

—¿Which one?

—Pick a Morales, any Morales. ¿Or how about the one the big sign out front is referring to?

—¿And who is inquiring?

I look around performatively. «Me», I say.

—¿Name?

—On behalf of Carlotta Ochoa.

—¿Is he expecting you?

—I have no idea what he's expecting, but if he's any good at deduction he should be.

—One moment.

She departs and I'm trying to figure out if this is a generalized antagonism or if I should be worried. I look out into the parking lot, catch Fercho then Mauro's eyes, and manage to signal to them to stay in the car but watch our interaction closely.

—¿I'm Morales, and your name?

—Thanks for your valuable time, I know you must be busy. The flow of the dead is constant.

—Regrettably, yes. ¿You are?

—Here to pick up Angelica Ochoa's effects.

—¿Really?

—¿Why so surprised? I was in the room when Carlotta spoke to you and said I would be coming by.

—¿Spoke to *me*?

—Yes, you. I recognize your voice.

—I see. You didn't let me finish. My surprise is at the irregularity of it all.

—¿Irregularity? ¿Are you saying you regularly bury books and letters instead of bodies?

—You're not from here, I'm guessing. ¿American?

—Maybe we can get to know each other someday. But *today* I'm not too bright and can focus on only one thing at a time. And I bet you know what that one thing is. Unless there's a problem.

I look out to the car and the two tense up.

Funeral guy says nothing, just stares. He's trying to figure out if he really wants there to be a problem.

—No, of course not, no problem. We're here to serve the client. And, of course, whomever they may designate as a proxy. ¿In this case, Mr. . . . ?

—Great, she'll be thrilled to hear it.

He goes to a nearby desk and without the slightest difficulty is able to locate a hardcover green book with a handwritten letter sticking out from inside, this despite the desk not exactly being the picture of organization. He turns it over to me.

I take out the note then quickly rifle through the book. It certainly skillfully pretends to be the collected works of the three famous Colombian poets and sisters Dorila, Elmira, and Hortensia Antommarchi. But it is pretend. Because the book has somehow been altered, at the printer level, of all things, so that, but for a few initial and closing poems, what is actually contained therein is a lengthy series of unattributed mathematical and scientific equations devoid of any explanatory language.

—¿Anything else of hers? —I ask.

—That is all Madam gave me, your prominence.

—¿Why, by the way? ¿Why did she give this to you?

—These are, hmm, delicate situations, when there's no body. We ask the client, if they wish, to give us a substitute, something intimate. Human beings need closure. The grieving process cannot commence meaningfully without it. You know, I presume, about the stages of grief.

—I know they're a bullshit invention, if that's what you mean.

—Seems in this instance her discovery of the note was actually the impetus for making arrangements. My understanding, and the widow Carlotta was crystal clear here, is that the ceremony will proceed in a few days, personal effects or no personal effects. That said, I would urge you to have these materials back in time for their burial. ¿Will you be joining us for the ceremony?

—I will not. ¿And surely you leave open the possibility of a joyous cancellation?

—¿And does your mercy expect that?

—¿Expect? That would be a strange expectation indeed. ¿But what are your thoughts on the subject?

—I wouldn't know where to begin on something like that. I don't know enough about the tragic circumstances.

—¿Or even if they're truly tragic, right? ¿Or do you know something I don't?

—No, only that we've never had one of these canceled, I know that. But, yes, you're right. We must leave room for God to work, it *could* be canceled, that is true.

—Yes, that's precisely what I meant. Good day, sir. And may the cycle of life continue to revolve in your favor. Oh, and tell your colleague I'll miss her inimitable warmth.

When I get back in the car, I find I've been demoted to the back seat.

—¿Success? —Mauro asks.

"Yes."

They're asking more, but I'm purely locked on to the video clip on my phone.

—Mauro, I just sent you a still photo of a license plate. ¿You got someone where they keep track of that shit can tell me who the car's registered to?

—¿How did you know?

—And that same place will have a facial recognition database. I just sent you a picture of the face driving that car.

—This is sounding expensive.

—I'm sure, but Carlotta just juiced us back up.

—¿Who's the guy?

—¿What guy?

—In the picture.

—¿You kidding? That's what you're going to tell me. ¿Could I have been clearer?

—No, I know. ¿But why did you take his picture in the first place?

—That's who was driving the car behind us when Fercho endangered our lives with his insane maneuver.

—¡You told me to!

—¿So?

—¿So Fercho did what he did, this guy was directly behind us, and not a peep of complaint? No horn, no profanity, nothing. Just takes his near-death experience in stride and continues on his merry way. ¿Sound like life in Cali to you two?

—Well, it is strange.

—¿Unless he was following us, right? Then it's suddenly not strange at all. Last thing he can do then is make a scene.

—¿In seriousness?

—"That birth product of a bad conception!"

—All right, then, let's not lose the plot here, gentlemen. Mauro, I just sent you two other pictures. One taken at *Cristo Rey*, the other at the zoo. Maybe same guy, maybe not. But either way, I need the same analysis.

—I know I'm late to all this, Riv, ¿but are you saying we're being followed?

—Just me, not we.

—So, ¿what now?

—This is good, drop me here.

—¿You're getting out? ¿Just like that?

—¿Is there another way? Be good, kids. I need to dive into this book and note. ¿Think you can get me answers by tomorrow morning?

—I do.

So that we all then agree to breakfast at *Simón Parrilla* the next morning. When maybe I'll be in a less combative state, events will cohere better, and the membrane between living and dead won't seem so fucking permeable.

23rd entry: the prosody of a death rattle

THE ARGUMENT

*Maybe all writing is testamentary. Either that or a
handclap of dust into a sandstorm.*

Dearest World,

*In the end, it's all mostly letdown. Isn't that always the way?
Life wants to default to a static nothing. But we who are cursed
with it can't abide that fact, so we counter with anticipation. We
anticipate a break in the monotony and only retrospectively do
we realize that the anticipation itself was the distracting event.
Because the nature of anticipation is to grow in quality while
the nature of whatever was anticipated is to steadily decrease in
appeal, starting the exact moment it terminates all anticipation
by actualizing. So the letdown sensation is just the casting
into stark relief of the fact that the primary element of life is
diminution.*

*I don't want to name this, but its nameless eyes see clear into
mine. I do want to escape this hovel of ill repute, escape from
responsibility.*

*"You say it's not the words so much as their shadows and
I remind you that shadows is just an evasive way of saying
darkness."*

There are consolations I suppose. How Luka Sorkočević can take you to Van Gogh who can take you to Crane and so on. The complexity of it all can be a type of solace. But isn't simplicity more genuine? If you were to strip away and strip away all the world's artifice, the primary remaining element would be authenticity, no? A single-celled organism is, more than anything, true. But to build a human being, mount lie upon lie.

You are changing me, you are the change. Only "I don't want to change, I just want change."

Failure. Weird noun where the more and more of it you experience, you suddenly become it. I am now a failure. The equations won't coalesce. You can make all the claims you want in this field. But intuition and logic only get rewarded when the math gets suggestive. So there's what I know is true but cannot prove and how that runs alongside the great many untrue things others have proven.

"This is another dark spiral I cannot break free of that I feel coming on." If you make everything you have, and are, about one thing, then when that thing disappears you are left with nothing. You are nothing.

You say hold my hand, then we'll grow up, then we'll grow, then.

Lives are a silly thing, but I can't live mine through another.

The absurdity of existence. Is it separable from the absurdity of choosing to continue to exist? Camus says the choice whether or not to continue is the primary question and I agree. But I think I disagree with his conclusion about this sad bone, this bad prison.

Arrange my scars the right way and they read like a constellation.

I know I told you I need to feel everything, but that was back when I could feel. Then the pain comes in and it just grows and grows off the very attempts to dull it until all there is is growth.

This is the sad truth. My entire life has been a form of endurance. I haven't really lived, I've endured. But endurance is a finite resource. It itself doesn't endure, it exhausts. And you can fight and fight the exhaustion to keep enduring, but only to a point. I can't fight any longer. But for this action, the sadness would last forever.

There is no blame. Certainly none for you, but not for me either. We can no more control who we are at birth than we can control how or where we're born. I was born me and that came with certain facts about how I would always baseline feel. A kind of prison.

It may also have come with a kind of clock on how long I would be able to bear these native injuries. But all that is distinct from the world within a world I was born into. A blameless collection of beauty I have nothing but gratitude for. This is an apology too. I no longer wish to add to the pain my coldness and neurological discordance cause, and this is the only way, because I can control neither.

My heart comes in parts, parts that don't fit, you can't fix it, true, but at least the devil can't break it.

I also won't add an ultimately grim discovery to the hurt I've spent a lifetime creating. I just go to join the water of the world instead. Quieting into silent disappearance instead of violent termination. A final token.

Finally, perspective best comes to our aid when it is general. This is a loss that will be felt by only you, and in a limited fashion for a limited time. And once you disappear, so will this injury that the remainder of the universe felt not one bit.

Because Hume was right, my absence will be felt by that entity no more than that of an oyster.

Warmly,
Angelica

24th entry: animal reason

THE ARGUMENT

To operate, logic needs facts, ideally actual ones, but provisional ones will sometimes do.

I picked *Simón Parrilla* for breakfast because I knew they'd be late and I at least wanted somewhere pleasant to wait. The place is all wide open but under a thatched roof, with giant charcoal grills all around and music from the roots of longing and . . . well, just a brilliant setting.

When they finally arrive there's no explanation for the lateness. I know because I listen carefully for one. I tell them it's customary to apologize and make with an explanation even if you have to stretch the truth a bit. They counter that that's not the custom. That the custom is to add twenty to thirty minutes to any time fixed by the parties to the fixing. And it's true that they're the authorities on customs where we are, so I laugh and tell them that if it's okay with them I'm going to pretend they hit traffic.

—¿What do you have for me, Mauro?

"The *buñuelos* are the best in the city."

—I was thinking more about the license plate from the car outside the funeral home and the face of the most patient driver in Cali.

"Ah, yes, per course. Here, now tell me I'm not the best."

—Okay, you're not the best.

"Oh no? Wait like you read my report. And, remember, there can be only one best."

—I'll remember.

I read.

—So car's registered to Leonides Velez and that's his face too. ¿Should that name mean something to me?

"Keep reading, cousin."

—¿This address mean something?

—No, but Fercho here had the great idea of having my man run the address itself in a bunch of databases.

—¿Nice, and?

"And guess what?"

—I don't want to guess, I want to spend that time and effort knowing.

—That license plate information was recently submitted to his local government by a Mr. Estevan Cuevas. Cuevas was seeking and received permission from his town to park that car overnight in front of his house. ¿Now why does Cuevas care where Leonides Velez, who lives seven kilometers away, parks his car? Well, look at the Cuevas address.

—Might answer your question.

—*Avenida de las Américas*. Let me guess.

—¿Thought you didn't like guessing?

—*Torre de Cali* vicinity. The Mondragon house the cop called from the payphone. No, the house with the green roof, the one at the end of the connecting tunnel, ¿right?

"Yes! Told you I was the best."

—You mean Fercho. Fercho's the best.

"Wait a minute."

—You're both the best, co-bests.

—There's more. ¿When do you think he applies for the parking pass?

—The day Angelica goes missing.

—¡Correct!

—¿Very meaningful, no? ¿Riv?

—Very.

—We know what it means, Riv. He smiles. —But maybe you could give us your interpretation so we don't dominate the conversation.

—Thank you, I hate being dominated. Here's one interpretation. Angelica is kidnapped by Mondragon people. She is not killed so she needs to be held somewhere. They decide to hold her in the house with the green roof, registered owner Estevan Cuevas. The place has to be fully manned at all times so reinforcements are stationed there to safeguard her. Velez is part of that reinforcement crew so he's going to be essentially living there and wants to be able to park in front.

—¡Wow, I think you're right! I mean, yes, that's what we were thinking.

—One interpretation, not *the* interpretation.

—There's no other.

—You didn't read her note. If you had, you would know.

—¿Know what?

—She killed herself.

25th entry: an elaborate lie

THE ARGUMENT

*Were truth not a fundament of the universe, there would
be no great sting to lying.*

In a life, some of its people are like art. Meaning we interpret
them. But we, the interpreters, change. And that affects the in-
terpretations. So with someone like my father, a man I stopped
experiencing directly at fourteen, what I see when I think of him,
or when a forgotten memory resurfaces, depends greatly on who
I am at the moment.

I think he wished everything was a lot more mysterious and
spectacular, my father. And it's not only that I didn't think that at
the time, it's that I wasn't even capable of thinking it then, if that
makes any sense.

But I had eyes and could see. And our apartment was full of
books on aliens, both their civilizations and their interventions
in ours. Others on the untapped potential of the human brain.
Also, advances in physics were laying bare how fundamentally
deceiving our physical world is. Not to mention inquiries on the
genuinely mysterious soul. The gist of it all was that heaven and
earth couldn't begin to cover all that needed explaining. Life was
a search.

All that could be mostly ignored by a kid. But also signifying mostly in retrospect is the constant moviegoing. One of the surprising features of that is how often it would be just him and me. I can only deduce this involved movies my mother had expressed no interest in and my sister deemed too young for. Not that this latter element seemed to play any appreciable role in anything, since often the best I could personally hope for once he selected the movie was apathetic confusion fostered by the glacial pace of seventies American cinema. So when I wasn't being actively psychosocially scarred, it seemed to me that this thing, movies, consisted mainly of adults talking to each other in a room, then others talking in a different room, and whoever engaged in the most conversations got the movie named after them.

Moving from the general into the specific, one such outing was a documentary on near-death experiences that went unduly heavy on the reenactments. Seems the subjects had been *Beyond and Back* and the grimly serious narrator was drawing conclusions that couldn't fail but impress a seven-year-old.

What came to me then was not any detail of the theatre or any particular behavior by either of us. What I remember is that near the end of the sober presentation things got even more real. The claim was that suicides were in for a particularly bad time following death. I don't recall much empirical support being marshaled in support of this claim, but I do remember the visual of malformed bodies clawing at a woman who'd tried to take control of her fate. Clawing desperately until she could finally escape and reenter her earthly body. And this is the kind of stupid shit enters my mind just then sitting with Mauro and Fercho.

And it's considerable stupidity too. If anything, someone so cursed from birth that they would irreversibly give in to their urge to immolate would, in a just world, be entitled to greater dispensation, not a continuation of their suffering. It can't be that it continues or worsens.

—¿You still with us? ¡Riv!

"Huh?"

—¿What do you mean, she killed herself?

—Her letter.

—¿What about it?

—Her letter is basically a suicide note.

—¿What?

—That.

—¿How is that possible? So beautiful.

—Beautiful woman.

—Not sure the relevance of that fact, but I am sure that's what the letter purports to be.

—Poor Carlotta. No wonder she suddenly dropped the whole thing. What a terrible development to confront.

—The act that runs most counter to God's plan —says Fercho.

—¿Why do you say that?

—The will of God.

—No, I'm looking for more analysis than that.

—¿So, Riv, this is over, then? It's hard to believe this all just disappears like that, one moment to the next. This is a true horror. I'm sorry I embedded you in this whole thing. ¿But why?

"Why what?"

"Why she do suicide?"

—She didn't.

—You just said she committed suicide.

—No, what I just said is that the Angelica letter Carlotta found is a suicide note.

—¿Yeah, and what follows those is suicide, no? One announces that the other is going to immediately follow.

—Not always, and not here.

—¿What are you saying?

—The letter is nonsense. No, I take that back. It has a great deal of sense, just that none of that sense truly relates to Angelica Alfa-Ochoa killing herself.

—¡Thank God! I hope you're right.

—I am, but I wouldn't go thanking anybody just yet. There are states worse than death. Even, contrary to Fercho here, the self-inflicted kind.

—¿Why do you doubt the letter? I assume she wrote in it that she was going to kill herself and she's been missing for almost a week. ¿Don't they teach Occam in the States?

—Probably not as well as here but not really applicable to our letter. Because this thing screamed fraud from the moment I heard of it.

—¿A lie?

—A thorough one.

"And you knew this and we still risked the life of our limbs to get it?"

—Yes, I needed it because, like a lot of thorough lies, it's full of useful truths.

—¿Like what?

—Wait, Mauro, first I need to know how it's fraudulent. ¿Why you think that, Riv, how you know it's a fraud?

—Normally I only do this for paying customers, but out of love and just this once, listen closely. When Carlotta first told me about the alleged letter from Angelica, she appended two main factual assertions: that she had only discovered its existence two days earlier and that she had discovered it where she keeps her photo albums. These two assertions were very nice in that they were very reliably true but also highly dissonant with each other. ¿A painstakingly composed final statement to the world that runs the risk of never being discovered? When I asked Carlotta what occasioned her going to that shelf, she pointed to an alumni re-quest for a photo of Angelica. This is laughable, though I'll admit the fake letter was pretty well done. ¿Also in that batch of mail incidentally? Advertising from that funeral home we visited. The kind of machinations you'd expect from a document that must be discovered but also cannot be in an obvious location if the days of delay are to be believed.

—¿I guess it could all be coincidence, no?

—Then there's the letter itself. It has zero ring of truth, like hearing a parrot tell Death to be not proud. It knows its true audience, in a damning way, and feels like boxes are being checked. The whole thing reads wrong, I'm saying.

—¿How?

—The prose was weirdly familiar to me for one. ¿Ever hear something and feel you've heard that specific syntax before but can't quite place it? A lot of that. It's all over the place. Allusive, derivative, familiarly unusual. ¿Who is she talking about? ¿Or to? ¿What's with the weird quotation marks that don't reference anything even mildly famous? There's no Angelica there is the bottom line.

—¿It's in English?

—English. ¿But that part's not surprising, is it?

—No.

—There's more, but it's so crazy I can't even say it out loud, so I'll stop there.

I certainly wasn't going to divulge that while reading the note I'd had the extreme yet hard-to-place sensation of repetition, even of being quoted.

—No, please. ¿What else?

—Just a little more, then. The physical letter itself is inauthentic. The paper doesn't match what's in the house. A clear effort has been made to make it look older. The ink is all wrong, effortful uniformity that doesn't happen with genuine letter writing. That'll have to do.

—I'm persuaded.

—Me too, on to the truths.

—¿The what?

—You said the letter was a lie but one that nonetheless revealed useful truths. ¿So what are those truths?

—Ah, right. The most salient truth, of course, is that some-one did all this. The letter's composition, the break-in to place it on the bookshelf, the *alumni* letter, the coordination to deliver it simultaneously with a brochure from that particular funeral home. These things all have an author or authors. We have well established that Mondragon's prints are all over this. But the good news is that Angelica herself must have at least contributed.

—¿Why do you say that?

—There's just too much about this development that could only exist due to her input. Think of knowing where Carlotta keeps her pictures for example. To contribute this way, you first have to be alive. So let's add that to what we know. As we sit here, it is overwhelmingly likely that Angelica Ochoa is still alive. Angelica lives.

—¿So now what?

—I'm going to go get her.

26th entry: the inactivity bias

THE ARGUMENT

The globe will rotate and revolve even in the perfect absence of human conduct.

Now the three of us are sharing something I can't remember us ever before sharing: extended silence. It's like in those horror movies where a character suddenly speaks the one verboten phrase. I have said, out loud, that I am done learning and reasoning and supposing and will now move on to action. And the reaction to this has been a kind of complete deflation. They occasionally look at each other but don't seem to want to meet my eyes.

—We shouldn't do that.

—I agree *we* shouldn't, Mauro. I said *I* was going to.

—That's crazy. Tell him, Fercho.

—You don't know, brother.

—I know enough. And that enough tells me it's time to act.

—¿But what do you really know? Because none of this makes a lot of sense.

—I don't need a complete understanding of everything happening to know next steps. What I know now will have to speak for the unknown.

—¿Like what?

—Like there are no complex human actions without motivation. The amount of planning and work that went into that suicide note farce can only mean genuine need on the part of her captors. We know Angelica is alive and we know where she is. But we also now know that, for whatever reason, they want Carlotta to give up hope. These people are not known for their subtlety, so if they at all could, they would make their point by sending her the head of her daughter. They don't because they can't, and they can't because they need that head to be alive and attached. They need Angelica alive because only she can do or disclose or teach or explain something, count on it.

—¡So she's safe!

—No, because second that service is fully rendered they'll expunge her.

—You don't know that.

—I absolutely do, and so does Angelica.

—¿Huh?

—Remember that she had to help with this death letter scheme. Maybe she used her leverage to try and put her mother out of the misery that is inchoate grief. But it's telling that she only did so in a way that assumes they will never see each other again. This is last-act-on-earth stuff, make no mistake. Above all is the notion that whatever this project is, it is something that can still be disrupted by nosy interlopers. We know they don't have to worry about the police, and Carlotta may seem a feeble adversary, but they strike me as take-no-chances people who just want to clean up this final detail.

—Look, I don't want to speak ill of the dead, or those soon to join them, but you never met Angelica. She wasn't exactly the warmest person.

—¿And if it's all such a farce why would Carlotta even believe it? —Fercho adds.

—There's no *why* here. People believe what they want to believe and she wants to believe this on some level, a sign of just

how horrible some of the alternatives are. ¿How convincing did
it really have to be? Conveniently written in English to be read
by a traumatized soul, there's enough distance there to ultimately
overcome any misgivings. Besides, ¿why am I even arguing on
behalf of its persuasiveness when it demonstrably worked? ¿Remember when she called off the investigation and invited me to
the funeral?

—¿So what's this project they need her for?

—¿Hell would I know? But it must pertain to her field or
maybe someone she knows in her field. I shouldn't say *must*. It
might have to do with some work of her father, ¿did he leave
some unfinished or unpublished work that she took up? Either
way, the details are far less important than the critical role she
obviously plays.

—So we know she's safe at the moment, let's figure out what
this project is and attack it from that angle.

—No, clock's ticking fast. ¿Look here, see the parking pass?
It expires in two days.

—¿So?

—So passes are available for up to thirty days but our henchman only requested ten. I've been watching the area and they are
preparing to travel. Two days from now she'll be either killed or
moved from that house to disappear into the giant darkness that
is the world.

"Wow."

—Forgive me, but even if everything you're saying is true.

—It is, Fercho.

—¿Does it necessarily follow that you should go get her?

This is all too much for Mauro:

—¿*Go get her*, Fercho? ¿Do you even hear yourself? You say
that like he's debating whether to pick up a new phone, like it's
something he can just decide to do. Please don't add to his severe misunderstanding of all this. ¿Riv, you don't just knock on a

Mondragon door, ask to borrow some *panela*, then throw in oh, would you mind terribly releasing your hostage?

—I agree, Mauro. ¿But even putting that aside for the moment, hasn't Carlotta terminated the investigation? All that stuff about her choosing to believe the letter and arranging a funeral. Riv no longer has a client.

—A minor detail.

—So even if it were feasible, ¿under what authority would you be claiming her?

—¿Authority? I claim nothing less than the ultimate authority. Ultimate to mean not just greatest, but also in its root etymological sense of final. Our final authority is issue of the authority of life over death, truth over lies. And we derive it not organically but negatively. By that I mean that whenever illegitimate power is exercised, the universe grants us the opposite power to author its disruption, and by whatever means necessary. The authority is universal in addition to being complete and final, because it is shared equally among opposers, invisibly distributed like air.

Think of the illegitimacy of the power exercised here. A man decides he needs something that a woman has or knows. ¿So what does he do? He plucks her off her vine and into his hand the way you might a spoilt strawberry. Plucks her out of her natural propriety to become just another plaything in his cellar. A *man* does this, nothing more than that. A little creature that shits and farts and picks its nose also creates terrestrial infernos. Tell you what, we'll countenance this when lizards start kidnapping fellow lizards. But that will never happen because this behavior belongs exclusively to the land of human activity, this is what the higher reason unique to humans is apparently for. Forget for now the evil of it all and think of the arrogance.

I'm going to take back what rightly belongs to our world while making sure this action of mine also takes the form of punishment. ¿Should we instead sit in perpetual wait, confident in eternal justice? God either refuses to act, or we invented him, or God has died.

—Careful, cousin.

Fernando's eyes are wide open.

—What best fills absence here is retribution —I say. —Mondragon's going to feel this. And when I pull him up, it'll be by the root to ensure no more life will ever feed this pestilent weed. So, yeah. I'm going to go get her.

—¡We need to go get her!

—I agree.

—¿But how?

27th entry: a novel plan

THE ARGUMENT

When a group endeavors to create something, it can sometimes be difficult to ascertain if the true motivation is the ultimate creation or the creative act itself.

—I said how, Riv.

—And I heard you, Fercho.

—He can't answer you because there is no answer. No *how* exists. What you are experiencing now, Riv, is the gap between intent and ability. You may very much want to go retrieve Angelica but no amount of *want* will change the fact that you have no genuine power here. On one side is one of the primary movers of evil the world has ever housed. On the other side is only the plain fact that there is no other side. There is no equal and opposite reaction to evil, only its victims.

—I don't know about all that, I just have some questions the two of you may be able to answer.

—¿And of course, Mauro, there is certainly a countervailing force to evil, you think God would permit differently?

—My questions are a lot easier than that —I say. —I'm wondering if we can very quickly gather a small group of hard guys to help on this.

—¿What do you mean by hard?

—Fercho knows what I mean. ¿True?

—True, but there's a problem, more than one. ¿What did you have in mind?

—Depends on what you see as the problems with acquiring them.

—Well, Riv, here's your problem. The group of potentially useful people I know breaks down along two main lines. The first group is probably what you're thinking of. They're highly skilled and professional. They've seen some shit and won't panic under pressure. The problem is they're also smart. That means that on the off chance Mondragon hasn't already gotten them under his control, either by employing them directly or indirectly, or his other forms of control, they're nonetheless too smart to knowingly go against him and way too smart to do so unwittingly.

—¡Think about that, Riv, too smart!

—The other group, cousin. This group is crazy, no better way to say it. Pay them enough, they'll do anything. They don't value life at all, including their own, because living the life they're chained to contains too little reward. They're crazy. Crazy as in the opposite of smart and crazy enough to not care about Mondragon. But you also can't collaborate with that kind of crazy.

—Got it, so I've been watching that house constantly and I also have an old blueprint I consult. I think I know what room they keep her in. ¿Is there an honest cop or military would extract her while I cause a big disruption at the front door?

—No.

—No.

—¿What if the gas company called them with news of a leak and an order to evacuate?

—Hmm.

—Don't know anyone in gas.

—Doesn't have to be genuine.

—None of that works, Riv, because we would lose the element of surprise, one of the few things we have going for us.

—Yeah, about that.

—There is no *element*, Fercho, that works to our benefit here. Riv talks about creating a distraction at the front door and you let him talk. That's lovely, reality is less so. Because second he gets within a hundred feet of that front door, there will be minimum five guns pointed at his head just in case.

—Maybe.

—And you'll know it's happening, Riv, because the hairs on the back of your neck will mysteriously rise.

—That part's true.

—So what you two are saying is that we can't enlist any effective help, legitimate or illegitimate. We are alone.

—Correct.

—That I can easily believe. And it's also true that where Angelica is being held is heavily fortified and that instigating anything out of the ordinary will only exacerbate their wariness. And I add that we have about forty-eight hours before something happens that will eliminate even the tenuous access we now have. In short, there is nothing can be done.

—That's true, nothing. There is nothing.

—Well, I agree, in a sense, but I have a plan.

—¿You have a way of overcoming all this?

—I didn't say that. I realize that when people say they have a plan it's generally implied that they think they have a good plan, one that at least hints at success. But that's not what I'm saying. I'm conceding that no plan based on force will work here. Leaving only subterfuge and its offspring.

—¡As in surprise! Everything we've said. ¿They never expect counters, especially small-scale ones, because who has the audacity?

—Actually, Fercho, I was going to say before. We don't have surprise on our side.

—¿What do you mean?

—¿Remember the part where we were undeniably followed to the funeral home?

—Oh, shit.

—Son of a . . .

—¿Or the many days predating that where I've been under constant surveillance?

—Wow.

—Or how we're being observed as we speak, though thankfully they can't hear us.

Second that escapes my lips is pure regret as they start frantically looking around.

—Please don't do that, gentlemen.

—¿So what do we do now?

—We do nothing. I mean that, this is critical. We'll part here and to all appearances have accepted Carlotta's cancellation. ¿Clear? Super important.

—¿That's the plan?

—It's a good plan.

—No, that's not the plan, it's a necessary prerequisite to the plan.

—¿Which is?

—Centered on intense bluffing and other deception and which can only be executed in person and by me.

—I'm going with you.

—You are *not* coming with me.

—I like the pretend plan better —says Mauro. —Let's not just appear to accept Carlotta's cancellation, let's actually accept it. Accept it and while we're at it, accept the way of the world. That evil goes unpunished and good rarely wins. Daughters don't get reunited with mothers and, no offense, private detectives don't stare down and outwit global criminal enterprises.

—Whatever is true generally, whatever the world's way, doesn't change our specifics: a terrified woman being bullied out of her humanity as prelude to losing her life.

—I agree with Riv. God put this in his lap for a reason. He cannot demur when it comes to the will of our heavenly father.

That said, Fernando excuses himself to the rest room while Mauro stares at me ruefully.

—Look, Fercho gets going on God's will and loses judgment really. People so want to believe everything happens for a reason. ¿I'm all for it too, but my point is if God cares so much about Angelica why involve us at all? ¿Why let her get snatched in the first place? Not to mention the literally millions of people whose deaths are attributable to this epic demon, nearly all of whom, I bet, cried out for help from that same God right to their very end. ¿Know what I think? I encounter someone doesn't believe in God, I don't judge, man. Seems reasonable if I'm being honest. After all, ¿what argues in his favor? ¿Where's the evidence? Now, Satan on the other hand. ¿How can you not believe in Satan? With him, all you have is evidence. The work of Exeter Mondragon alone more than proves the case. Visible actions that tangibly change our world, both our physical one and the ethical cosmos above it. Actions that taken together form a kind of diabolical worship. Proof. Precisely what's missing for the other side, which is why we're reduced to belief while they get to just passively observe.

—Jesus Christ, you guys.

—And you propose simply walking in there against that.

—Well, it's more complicated than that.

—¿Armed with what? ¿The grace of God? Here, everything is commended to that invisible force, but ask those millions where it got them. Drop this, cousin. You're only one person, and a blameless one at that.

—Your objection is noted.

—Most importantly, if you choose to go anyway, against my advice, I am going with you.

—Untrue.

Fercho returns.

—¿So what's our next move?

—Same as before you left. We go our separate ways for now. No contact of any kind, assume everything is tapped and that you're being surveilled. Let me look into some things, then I'll come to you tonight at nine. Until then, stay safe and try not to think of the unquenchable edacity of the murderous entity watching your every move.

28th entry: silence as signal

THE ARGUMENT

But for human imagination fueled by memory, we could almost lapse into a pleasant reverie.

That afternoon when I get back to the hotel I feel copious eyes on me as I stand in the lobby. And I'm peripherally aware that some of them belong to a very familiar face. I turn to look at these eyes and they belong to Carlotta. She sits in one of the lobby's plush chairs and she looks up at me from her magazine. I hold the look for a bit, trying to judge whether she knows we're being watched. We still on the same team? I walk to her, weighing my every coming word.

—¿This your favorite hotel too?

—It's haunted —she says as her eyes sadden.

—I know.

—So it can't be your favorite, then.

—No, *therefore* my favorite. ¿Why should I fear ghosts? A ghost is proof that it doesn't all just end here, transcendence.

—¿What if I want it to end, Riv?

—Fair point.

—I guess this is the end for us.

—Tell you what, Carlotta, my love. ¿See that pretty bench in the courtyard? Let's talk out there. That way if no one from in here follows us, we'll know it's a private conversation.

—¿Why would anyone follow us?

—They would follow us because I'm paranoid and the paranoid are constantly proven correct.

We walk there, seemingly unfollowed, but I watch a guy in the courtyard take a call, hang up with unnatural quickness, then come nearer to where we sit.

—¿Do you have the death letter, my son?

—I do, here it is.

—¿Now do you see my tragedy?

—I do, loss is . . .

—But sincerely I ask your forgiveness.

—¿Freely given, but for what?

—Because I'm sorry, in a sense, that I ever involved you. Especially since by the time I did it was already too late.

—¿Hmm, how are you coping?

—Better, I think, now that I have certainty.

—Explain.

She looks away from me and whispers absently:

—The certainty, it helps.

—I see.

—Maybe, Riv, life just cannot be squarely confronted sometimes. ¿You ever think of that?

—Often.

—And maybe we can never really know what's happening in the mind of another. Those are hidden universes within our visible one and there's no possibility of passage. So whatever the true facts are here, where we are, the explanation will always be locked away in that special place that's now even more inaccessible. I can't keep banging my soul against that door, begging for an entry that will never come. ¿Understand?

—I think so.

—Anyway, this obviously concludes the job you were hired to do. I want you to know that I appreciate all the hard work you did. I saw it, even if ultimately it must feel so empty.

—Only if everything is empty. If not, then this was among the richest work I've ever done.

—It was so silly to think God sent you. Even if I thought it, I shouldn't have said it aloud. It was unfair of me to put that on you.

—I don't know.

—So you see now why I have to end this. Take this final payment, it's more than we agreed to.

—Okay.

She's crying, I never know what to do.

—Time —I say.

—Yes, time.

Some passes.

—Riv, my heaven. ¿Will you be at the funeral?

—No.

—I'm not giving up, don't think that. There's a lot, I think, a lot I think, but not giving up is my overriding point.

—In every sense of that, you can be sure I agree with you.

—But reality cannot be negotiated with. You're looking at the funeral the wrong way.

—I'm not judging or interpreting it or anything else. It's just that, as you say, the job is done. So I'm flying back to New York tomorrow. I have obligations there.

—Oh, I see. I almost said I was sorry to see you go, Riv, but I realize that's not true. Anyone you meet during a terrible time becomes tainted by that and you never really want to see them again. It's not personal.

—I'm not offended. And if we ever see each other again maybe it'll somehow be about peace and love.

—Maybe.

—And if not, let's at least enjoy this moment. A moment where such a thing still seems at least possible.

29th entry: goodbyes are a form of death

THE ARGUMENT

You often know when you are about to stop seeing someone, it is always true that you do not know if you will ever see them again.

After separating from Carlotta I go back into the hotel lobby to loudly tell the front desk I will be checking out the next morning and will need a car to the airport, that sensation of speaking to many through one.

Because she asks, I announce that my working vacation is done and that I must return to New York. When asked to characterize that work, I add that it has been an abject failure. That maybe all human activity is.

Later I will go to Fercho and Mauro and repeat this lie. Now, I need . . . not sure what I need. After tomorrow, I will not be able to just decide, on a whim, to see a specific portion of Cali. I catch a cab and go north.

I go to church. The church has existed since the 1600s. But it's also not clear that anything physical I'm seeing actually dates back to that time. Maybe some of it, I don't know, but I'm getting a definite Theseus's Ship vibe. It's the name makes it so, it seems. Once a group decided this enclosure was *Iglesia la Ermita* then entropy could have its way all it wants, but as long as humanity responds appropriately, the named entity persists. This naming is the only pure dominion we are given over the physical world and it now seems a paltry one. I'm reminded of the Holy Roman Empire that, Voltaire was right, was neither holy, Roman, nor an empire.

Still, it is undoubtedly a visual marvel. I will go inside and the people in there with me, mass or no mass, will whisper arguments for something more permanent than any name. And, who knows, they *could* be right. In case they are, I will ask for mercy.

But turns out I won't. The church is closed. Not only are all the doors closed and stonily resistant to movement, they all lack even handles.

I wander away, certain there's been a mistake, certain it will remain uncorrected. I am in *Parque de los Poetas*, only I don't see any poets anywhere. No evidence even that poetry is a thing.

At the edge of the park I decline into the Cali River, down in that river to pray.

It runs and runs and, yes, it will drain into the Cauca River of Death. We still call it *running* even though from a historical perspective, the word is hardly justified. Right now the water barely flows where I bet one day its manic profluence made it feel as if Life itself could never be contained. But *one day* excludes today and today it crawls, not runs, toward dusty death.

Does a river, one as central as this, have a memory of sorts? I think of its formation, the formation of all our rivers. The way rivers are just the end of a descent.

Flying over from New York, out the window, hours of ocean. What is more fitting than the wet truth that our world is mostly water, but of course only the kind that cannot be directly imbibed or used to promote the growth of human sustenance?

Fresh water on the other hand. Why every river starts as a river of life. Formed by the law that everything on Earth wants to fall to its middle. Descending from mountaintops to sprout cities and civilizations then, here, the kind of radical departures from civility that

fill and stop the waters with the weight of our dead. From mountaintops, meaning from the sky before that. Another way of saying
that our rivers are heaven-sent. And this is what we make of them.

That night I meet up with everyone on the occasion of it being
the last night of the calendar year and my last night in Colombia.
Amid fireworks and flying cork, my aunt Fanny wants to know
why I'm going back so soon. I tell her that from my perspective
it feels like the opposite, that events from before I landed in Colombia may as well belong to a different century. Then I tell her
about seeing her face again after so many years. That maybe every
lifetime gets twenty or thirty powerful faces and hers was one of
them for me.

Fercho and Mauro arrive together and corner me forthwith.
They're the picture of maudlin concern. Because I'm leaving? Because I might not? I think it's one of those situations where everyone intuits but won't say out loud that there's been an irreversible
development that radiates harm and now it's just a question of
fixing the degree.

—You're going home, I wish we'd had time to arrange a better
send-off. This guy, he leaves and takes the year with him.

—I just remembered, tomorrow is Angelica's birthday —
Mauro adds.

—Seeing you guys again, truly amazing.

—That's right. She was born at 12:00:01 am on the first day of
2000. Strange thing to know, but Carlotta would always let drop
that Angelica was *the* millennium baby.

—Seems a fair thing to highlight.

"But, Riv, *porque* the change in mind?"

—You said it yourself, many times, there's nothing more I can do.

—Sure, I've been saying it plenty. The novelty is you now
saying it.

—¿You're saying what, she's dead?

—I didn't say that, Fercho. She may be, but what I said was there's nothing more I can do, which I think was Mauro's message all along.

—Because it's the truth. Even so, I'm interested in how you came to recognize my wisdom.

—Yeah, earlier today you said she was alive, convinced us, and implied a plan was in the works. ¿What changed?

—Carlotta came to my hotel. She fired me.

—I'm sure she didn't mean it that way.

—There was nothing contentious about it, you see. But unemployment is one of those things that speaks for itself. So none of this is any more of my business, literally.

—She thinks her daughter's dead.

—I agree she thinks that, but I also think it's less a conclusion than an act of will.

—¿You agree with her?

—She's the client. And besides, *who am I* is I think Mauro's greater point. And come to think of it, maybe Carlotta's point as well. ¿So does it ultimately matter what I believe? ¿What can I do about my beliefs? There is the question. ¿If one of the world's primary movers of malevolence . . .

—No, malevolence itself.

—is arrayed against us, then who am I? ¿Tell the authorities? He owns every last one of them. ¿Bring greater force than his to bear? ¿How exactly? ¿Deception and nerve? Those are poor weapons compared to lead and gunpowder.

—Stay just a bit longer —Mauro says. —Go to the funeral, everyone will feel better after the funeral.

Fernando's mouth opens silently, then:

—Let's say you *were* going to do something for Angelica. ¿What would you do? I know you've thought about it.

—I'm not going to do anything except fly back to New York tomorrow.

—Hypothetically then.

—Hypothetically only, I would go straight to where she's being held. Not that I think it's the most brilliant idea, but desperation moves are all that remain. I would go there and just disrupt. When orderliness and structure are choking the life out of you, cause chaos.

—¿Could it work?

—Anything *could* work. But probably the only result would be the quick end of your favorite agent of chaos.

—Maybe so, but if you go, we go.

—Yes —says Mauro.

—I'm *not* going, that's why I called it a hypothetical.

—¿Promise?

—Besides, me going would be drastically different from you two going.

—¿Hell's that mean?

—Nothing.

—¿No, what?

—Let's face it, men. You have lives, responsibilities. I have nothing. Which means nothing has me. You two can pay the price of your own actions, but if you think I'm facing your wives and kids after you've faced the price of mine.

—That's crazy.

—More than anything it lacks relevance —I say.

Then come the grapes. If you eat grapes on New Year's Eve it ensures that the ensuing year will be rife with success in every possible way that word signifies for you. And the first time you hear this kind of especially Colombian supernatural assertion you laugh. The next time you giggle then maybe you smirk. Problem is, by the millionth time you hear something like this stated as incontrovertible fact, you can't help but abandon reason and un-critically absorb it all until you simply jump ahead and conclude that the rules are just different here than they are in, say, Times Square, New York. I eat a lot of the grapes is what I'm saying.

Then I posit a solution:

—Let's open this bottle, ¿yes? Everything will make more sense once we pour this into our bloodstreams. ¿Ready? ¡To doing nothing!

And we raise our glasses to the sky.

Sky because by then we are outside in a little patio.

And anyone looking down from above would mistakenly think we had accomplished some sort of finality.

last entry: a special heat death

THE ARGUMENT

All the world's individual human arcs ultimately cancel each other out, leaving only the arc of the universe.

The next morning I am not sharp. I kind of look sharp, though, with my green cowboy hat and matching green sunglasses. I sit in the lobby until the woman at the front desk informs me my car has arrived.

I walk to the driver and, after confirming that the hotel called him, tell him there's been a mistake. See, I forgot the hotel had made arrangements and made my own. But today's your lucky day. Because here is cash payment in full for a trip to the airport that will actually be provided by another who, oh look, there he is now.

He is looking around not knowing what to do, confirming everything I feared, basically. I ask him if he's looking for someone and he's forced to say no. He takes the money without thanks and drives away. I hurry into the other car and get it going. I see that the original driver has stopped about a block away and gotten on his phone.

My new driver is a gift. His foot is heavy and his mouth is closed.

Later, as we pull into a parking garage at my direction, I have a question for him.

—¿See that guy over there?

He does and when I ask if the guy looks like me at all he displays surprise that, yes, he actually does. He's growing curious, but I exit the car to address my replacement who, to me, looks nothing like me. I give him my hat and sunglasses and ask him to again repeat his instructions.

It's simple, he says. He will not ever take off the hat and sunglasses until the job is done. He will check into the airport as this Riv character. Only once he is in the area restricted to ticketed passengers will he cancel his flight. Then he will closely observe if that cancellation seems to give rise to any unusual activity. If satisfied it hasn't, he'll discard the hat and glasses, destroy the phony paperwork, and return to his life. With heavier pockets, thank you.

Is that accurate? I say it is. But that I hope the flippancy with which it was just now relayed is indicative of his mastery over the material and not a mistaken belief that the details are susceptible to even the slightest variation. Because they are not.

They leave, the driver and replacement Riv. I see what I want to see in response and go to the nearby car I've rented. It speaks, this car. It says the drive to Mondragon will take thirty-three minutes.

I'm about a block from my destination when I see this world's worst sight yet. I don't want to believe it, not truly. But there's no mistaking the car I'm looking at. Whatever the reason in our omnipresent hell, Mauro or Fercho, or both, have come to this maledicted location where air goes to die. And they are not in the car, so whatever this is, it's too late to not be it.

No time for suspense to build. My phone buzzes and it's Mauro.

—Cousin, I know you're at the airport. Too late to come back, ¿right?

—¿Why would I come back?

—¿Too late, right? It's to say . . . we're at *Torre de Cali*, ¿can you come?

—¿Who's we?

—Fercho and I.

—¿Are where?

—*Torre de Cali.*

—¿Why?

—Yeah, like we discussed. Fercho has this crazy idea, something that's never been done before. He's going to start a traveling soccer team.

—Oh, God.

—It's never been done before. There's a guy here can help.

—¿Why?

—No, I understand, it's too late.

—Don't say that. I was crystal clear I would be at the airport, Mauro, for hell's sake. That I was done with all this.

—I know, forget it, we tried.

—I'm here. ¿Understand? I'm coming to you.

—¡No! I mean, ¿isn't it too late?

—Both are true. I'll be there shortly *and* it's too late.

—¿So you comprehend?

—I do, forgive me.

—Then don't come, don't make it worse. What's done is done. And the line cuts off.

I perform the fiction so weakly that I lose the truth. I enter the lobby of the tower after delaying the appropriate time and, look at me, I'm the picture of innocent expectation, an individual who suspects exactly zero foul play.

Two burly guys immediately get up close and personal. They want to know if they can help me. I say they cannot, but turns out it wasn't a genuine question because now they are forcibly guiding me toward a door whose existence seems to materialize magically.

Then down more stairs than seems possible and through another door that opens into a long tunnel.

It's a tunnel to nowhere, this thing, and we walk and walk, but neither of my escorts says a thing.

And even now, or maybe now more than ever, this tunnel is returning me to something elemental. I grew up near a famous tunnel and, pile the information on all you might, I'm not sure I've ever gotten over the fundamental absurdity of it all.

If the tunnel bored through a mountain then that's the process killed John Henry and that loss hit me hard. If, like the one in my childhood, the tunnel connected two landmasses separated by deep water, that was even worse. Because how is it even possible to go from no underwater tunnel to staring at the walls from inside one for any sign that the relentless tonnage of water enveloping us is starting to break through?

The instant tunnel is of a species new to me. It is not evidence of any kind of collective will to progress. There's nothing official-seeming about it. It feels like the will of something individuated. And as if passage is from one secret to a deeper one. The claustrophobia of it, the tube of life is either constricting as we go or it only seems so; but it is immaterial which is so because, here, seeming makes it so.

"Thanks, fellas. But it seems to be getting tight in here. Why don't you two go on without me? I insist, no need to thank me."

That doesn't happen. But just as the pressure on my lungs grows intolerable, there emerges greater light. From halo to luminescence until I'm thrown into an empty room with concrete walls, no windows, odd light sources, and a long rusted metal chain and hook that hang down from the center of the ceiling.

"That does it, I'm calling the police on you two fellas. Kindly direct me to the nearest phone."

"We are the police."

They turn and leave to great laughter, always happy to amuse.

I am alone. I try both doors but there's no give. The chain and hook don't come off. There's nothing else in the room, nothing I could arm myself with, just the nothing I came in with.

Alone.

Jane was alive, is now dead, and I've not been fully either since.

I sit and wait for what's next.

It will come when it comes and it will be followed by more Nothing.

ZERO

Dawn to dusk to dark to dawn again, the way birth initiates life until death and any possible rebirth, just as any thesis has to give rise to its antithesis before an ultimate synthesis. The way of the world is for everything that lives to be both growing and dying at the same time. And the notion that nothing is ever truly destroyed, only transformed.

I was born half a century ago in Jersey City, New Jersey, and that very moment began wondering why.

Is this memory, dream, dream of a memory, memory of a dream? Because the irreality of it now.

To live, even briefly and retrospectively, in a world where you don't yet have the power of speech, is to exist as a kind of perfect victim.

My earliest visual memory is of my mother hovering over me and she wants me to wake but it's solely the surrounding aural and visual clues that make me understand that's what her words mean.

Then later, being alone. Being in danger. These are states words don't have to be put to. But not being able to do so back then only added to the terror. Realizing you are alone in an apartment having only recently acquired the ability to walk.

This was a sign. The moment of your birth is fundamentally deceitful. Were you to truly experience it, you could be forgiven for concluding that you'd just been born into a world of great solicitous attention and fulfilled anticipation. Better to learn, even at age one, the greater truth: that we are, every one of us, alone and in danger.

At fourteen I watched my father get lowered into the ground and wondered, given the magnitude by which the dead outnumber the living, how we hadn't yet run out of room. Later that year I saw the least handsome drowned man in the world, in the Florida everglades of all places, and sensed a solution.

Before my first quarter century I was engaged to be married while working simultaneously toward a law degree and a PhD, then I was none of those things and since then all things all at once and all the time.

Just before escaping to Colombia, my sister Genevieve was on the phone, not sure what to make of my plans except to demand and receive my promise that I would be careful.

Today I have all the words for being alone and in danger and even for staring down the ultimate irreality. But I will use none of them. Instead it'll all end the way it began, in a dimension alien to language with a primal mixture of incomprehension and resignation.

When the door finally reopens, in comes a terrible beam of darkness. From within it and out into the light emerge two figures. These are not the guys who had deposited me there. But I'm pretty confident they're not there to help me either.

They have badly scarred faces they seem eager for me to see. And the one doing all the talking speaks a rough Spanish that aggresses every syllable. This roughness or whatever makes it so I can't access what he says directly but instead must first translate it in my head.

—You don't look fancy. ¿What's so fancy about you?

The other one seems purely uncurious.

—I'm quite fancy. Fancy enough that you need to escort me out of here before you get yourself in even worse trouble.

He smirks and turns to the other. «¿*Te imaginas el patrón?*» And the other seems to imagine just that before showing more of his face as answer.

—That's exactly who I'm thinking of, your boss. I know him very well, certainly better than you do, and I know he's going to be quite upset when he sees what you've done.

—¿What we've done? We do his will. ¡In all things his will!

—Fine, but before you can do someone's will you must first interpret it properly. So, consider, ¿when he was telling you I was fancy, wasn't that a signal that you should defer to me? ¿Isn't he fond of these little tests of someone's initiative when considering who to promote and who to punish?

They let go of me and look at each other. I keep nodding yes and leaning in the direction I came in, like a plant seeking the sun. They lean with me and momentum builds toward my freedom until . . .

—¡Wait!

They put their hands back on me.

—He didn't say you were fancy or special. We *guessed* that because he told us to bring you inside and no one ever comes inside. Said you were here about the other two.

I'd forgotten, the whole facing-death thing and all.

—¿Where are they? The other two.

They look at each other and laugh.

—Okay, then, take me to him.

—No, you should first understand how lucky you are.

—I understand.

—¡Of course you do! You are about to interact with *Exeter Mondragon*. ¿Do you even appreciate it?

—I just said I did.

—This is the greatest man alive, no, *ever*. ¿Do you know why you were put on this earth? ¿The reason?

—¿Punishment?

—You don't know the reason, no one does. But we do. If you are blessed enough to serve under Mondragon you know why you were put on earth and you know it every second. When he speaks . . . you just . . . know. You will soon understand.

—¿When is that? ¿He's going to talk to me?

—¿Haven't you been listening? ¿Why you're so lucky?

—¿What's he going to say?

—Whatever in hell he wants, ¡be sure of that! What matters is he'll be saying it *to you*. And you will somehow have the ears to listen to it. Understand that when we come into this room, it's already over. But not this time. *Bring it to him alive* we're told. ¿So what makes you the exception? Not that it matters, it won't change the nature of this room. ¿Do you sense it? Terrible things have happened here.

—Yeah, this is Earth. Something terrible has happened on every single scrap of it.

—¿See that chain with the hook?

—Hard to miss.

—What's left of the bodies hangs from there or covers the floor and we have to disappear it all, make the room look like this again. Add all the body parts together that we've handled and you could fill a small stadium. Look at the hook.

I look at the hook, why on earth am I following an instruction like that?

—The clarity of the man. *Clarity*, that's the word. So many people, this is the last room they ever see. But you, you get to see *him* before you die. I hope you appreciate the grace the universe has shown you in this eventuality. To be in the presence of that kind of *clarity*, even if only once.

I look around the room but can't really see anything anymore.

Instead I hear things. I hear a slow swell of past tense screams. They approach the room in the early stages of a doppler effect. But before it can all culminate I am pulled out of there and to a nearby staircase that we then ascend together, but with me as their cargo.

After a painful bit we are somehow out in the street. The air and the sun are welcome, but even more than that the visibility. People are around. Surely they will register my status as a captive. One or all of them will interfere and I will profit from the disruption.

But no one does. I was right about the readily apparent nature of my captivity but wrong that it would have any effect. Worse, the inaction was not due to any apathetic indifference. No, my sense was that everyone I saw, whether foreground or scenery, was somehow in on it all. That Mondragon owned far as the eye could see, owned every object, and people were just another form of object.

I think how it could be worse. But I often do that. Or, more accurately, will often will myself into that mode of thinking. Things will take a dark turn and before the movement is even complete I am drawing comfort from an imaginary state of facts that rightfully should have no real-world relevance. Except they do. They do and I'm not alone in this. So if imagination can serve this purpose, why? What is it about that tool?

Let's say there's two primary things imagination can do in these moments to help. You can fantasize about something positive to, in a sense, experience it and derive some of the benefit. Or you can use your imagination to do the whole it-could-be-worse thing I am currently doing. But that relies on an understanding that the imagined *worse* won't actually be occurring. In other words, what really provides solace is not the notion that *it could be worse* but rather the relief that *it could have been worse*, a pretty critical distinction.

Here, imagination is no comfort. Because no amount of it can distract from what is coming. And no grim counterfactual to my current state is at a safe enough remove. Imagining the most terrible events now feels a hell of a lot more like anticipation than relief. Meaning it will do no good to repeat any truism about the potential for worse. That would only mask the more obvious and inexorable truth: everything is about to get much worse and in a way that exceeds even my darkest imaginings.

My death will not reverberate widely. It will mostly be my sister Genevieve in pain. She'd expressed doubts about the whole affair. I gave it not enough thought for that. Just autopilot on to a plane to get as far away from the Jane mess as possible. Away from specific death but toward its apogee. And like the first global circumnavigators, I had gone way off into the distance only to end where I began: lamenting the lost, but ready now to join them.

But before that there's a lot these two want me to experience first. As we approach the green-roofed house I had once fixated on via video I see that the roof isn't green at all. Or it is green but not really a roof. It isn't the same house is the explanation. It's the same all right, but it isn't a house. And that isn't green or any other color. It is death if death were a color. Not the color that most approximates death or even the color that death would choose to represent itself. No, *death* is what you would utter if this entirely new color were suddenly discovered and you were tasked with naming it.

Whatever the structure's true nature, these two approach it as if it were a particularly meaningful place of worship. With disdain, they inform me that they are not allowed in, as if they expect me to help solve their problem.

—So . . . simple . . . let's not enter.

—*We* are not going to enter, you are.

—¿Or else what? You can't force me in without going in yourself. Smiles. Ugly crooked ones.

—You can't kill me if I refuse to enter, I bet interest in me is too high for that. And before you say that you'll just maim me, understand that I will make it so you have to kill me. No, I believe we'll just have to part ways here.

—Fine, we are in accord —says the quiet one. —¿Where you going? ¿Which direction? We're not going to touch you anymore. Better start running. Go.

He has a point.

—Run until you are completely beyond his reach. ¿Need directions?

I look around, but subtly. I am like a master of misdirection. But with mastery over no one or thing and quickly vanishing sights.

—I've *decided* to go in —I say. —Make sure you remember it that way.

—We will never see you again —says one.

—Or remember this in any way —adds the other.

The steel stairs to the door scale only upward. When I realize this, I try to reverse events and retreat downward. But there's no retreat possible because a stair, once fully ascended, dissolves into nonexistence.

On the other side of the door is a long hall. Or more like the sense of one. Because the only light source is the one I just interrupted, and it loses influence the farther out I cast my eyes.

I decide that's it for me. I won't be moving forward in any way. Up ahead is nothing. No revelation or insight. No progress or regress, just stasis. There is nothing more I need to learn about the world that I haven't already learned from five decades of being assaulted by it.

Except it turns out it's not about any of that. I had sensed more choice than was truly present. Because where I stand is a spasm. One that impels me forward. And not like any natural process. Like a foreign object being mechanically excreted.

I come to a room on my left, there is only left now. The darkness lifts as if I were light itself and I begin to make out a figure. Not a human, a figure. It is writhing. Maybe. Or is it the special light coming and going that makes it seem so?

I stare.

It isn't human because of the hair, hair like fur like on a beast. I stare.

Then I hesitate toward the figure. And the light shifts and shifts to reveal, piecemeal, different aspects of the vision. The hair, yes. But also its movements are inhuman.

Will I draw closer? I will. Only to confront my error. That isn't hair, for example. They look like dark red staples. Attached violently and everywhere to the skin of, yes, a human. A circle of a human.

I make out that the circle is involuntary. The man before me forms a zero. His upper half bowed forward but his legs bent so extremely the wrong way that his feet arc backward to meet his forehead. At this apical juncture his head and feet have been sewn together, the thread some kind of steel wire. The same wire sews shut the holes where his arms had been. And at the core of it all a large metal razor ring holds everything in place.

I had been right at least about the movement. It isn't human. It is angular/inertial. Gravity pulls the human wheel forward. But only far enough to cause sufficient countervailing force to then pull the whole thing back. And on and on in a self-sustaining loll.

There is other movement too. I see that the staples are translucent. Translucent with movement within that I eventually recognize as slow but discernible blood flow.

I admit I froze in place.

This is . . . it feels like literal nonsense. But at the same time I recognize that it makes all the savage sense in the world.

I am reduced to an entity that can say nothing of the present, only detect change. So I sense minutely that the blood flow has stopped. And, oh, the grisly relief I feel just then on the level of my DNA.

But then it resumes, the flow of blood. As with anything destructive the globe over, any respite was only temporary. Now every displaced corpuscle testifies to that fact.

I hear a faint buzzer. But not a finite or intermittent one, a low steady buzz. I move toward it, farther into the dark, blindly guided only by this sound.

I have this odd sensation just then that the sound is, more than anything, kinetic. That there is no singular source, but rather a maelstrom of sources striving for primacy.

And a giant egg shape at the center. The egg as birthplace for life, but this one devoted to its opposite. It is a solid, I feel, even as its component molecules furiously redound into chaos.

Setting is everything. You can stare and stare at the most familiar visual concepts and still fail at recognition. Until I realize it is the unfamiliar pairing of familiarities that has stopped me. In this case a human body topped not by a head but by an active beehive.

Had the hive been grafted onto a decapitated body? I wish. The decomposing flesh and dried blood at the core of the seething mass meant something even worse. A different man, so not the one who'd been sewn into a human circle, had endured, for some time now, a beehive helmet that surrounded and feasted on his head.

I recoil, this time at the realization more than the sight. But I also need to know if I have to help or if this is all past tense. So I move closer. Closer means the noise swells and burrows into my brain so that thoughts have nowhere to form amidst the infernal buzzing.

Then the darkness becomes so complete I lose even those senses not dependent on light. A perfectly black and silent void that argues against the existence of anything, including existence.

Now, suddenly, light so bright and immanent it lands like pain. Well played by God or Mondragon or imagination. Shine a bright enough light on Everything and it dissolves into Nothing. From that perceptual nullity the incipient ray of night in the distance is like a beacon to otherhood. And anything is better than the present, so I follow this beam of black. That grows into a shaft. That leads me from that place. To follow the darkness.

The black deepens and deepens until resolving into a tube just big enough for me to stand and walk in. Big enough for that but not much else and I suddenly recognize the claustrophobe's truth. An infringement on your immediate space is an infringement on your right to breathe.

The growing tightness of it all. I know that return or even just turn is impossible.

Move my legs forward without reward. Walk and walk but my position is unchanged. It's all like a memory of a dream of being on a perpetual motion treadmill so finely calibrated not one centimeter of progress can be made regardless of any human effort. Still, I persist.

Now it's vertigo. Still walking but the only motion I sense is decidedly *not* of my body moving forward against a static backdrop. Instead, it's that the world keeps spinning. But not the world. Just some insane tunnel some of the world's people built within it during its winding history. And now that world's inalterable past will include this bizarre mechanical rotation of this tunnel's outer shell as I impotently try to push forward.

The disorientation is extreme, as if my neurons are carbonated and being shaken in a can. It lessens a bit when the treadmill effect finally ends and I begin to advance. But now the spinning speeds up. I'm in a centrifuge is what it is.

That means my components are being pulled apart. My heart is out of time again. I drop to my knees and start to crawl, crawling like a child.

And when I was a child it became fashionable to hang strings of beads in doorways in place of doors. In a mystical sphere I now access, I can see the vibrant colors and hard roundness of those long-gone beads with the force of current reality.

I was a child then and everything seemed mainly unreal as too new. Now, nearing the end of this our journey, I am again staring at a door of beads. Only they're not beads exactly, they're something more elemental. I am on my hands and knees like a penitent supplicant and pray to know what's before me before I dare traverse it.

Elemental all right. In place of round plastics, the curtain I'm touching arrays human bone. I know they're human because I'm full of them. It's the *why* that escapes me, until I push through to the room. A room that makes a bone curtain seem almost apposite.

At first, it's all just more confusion. The room is full of people who all look identical. No, the room is overfull of me, probably the last person I want to see right now.

How is this so? Everything in the room is glass, either mirror or window. That means all the room's light is either being reflected or refracted with reflections of refractions leading to refracted reflections or reflected refractions in a continuous loop. Like a snake swallowing itself by the tail while regenerating at the exact rate of consumption. I am the snake and I am everywhere.

At a distance I think I see the only stable independent image. I take three steps and I am there, the distance had been an illusion.

A man or something sits in a lush black chair and he extends his hand to invite me onto a nearby stool. I sit as he comes into focus. The sensation is of something going from gas to solid. It is a man, but unlike any I've ever before seen.

Or maybe not a question of sight or appearance, this is unlike any *presence* I have ever encountered. I'm looking around trying to determine how it manages to avoid the whole reflection/refraction business when it speaks, surprising me with faintly Oxbridge English.

"How do you like it?"

The timbre is orchestral.

"How? Not at all," I manage.

"You should try to extract whatever small pleasure you can from this setting. This is the last room you will ever occupy."

That feels true. He is looking at me and starting to smile.

"What are you doing here?" he continues. "Or, better yet, what is it you think you are doing here?"

"You don't know?"

"Let's pretend."

So much about this figure was opaque. For example, even sitting ten feet away, I still couldn't be sure what he looked like. But at the same time, everything about him that wasn't physical felt wholly transparent. It was as if his will were perfectly visible and there was no meaningful distinction between that will and future events, nor would there ever again be because that was his will. In the air, then, was whether ensuing events would be sufficiently interesting to this will to be suffered by it.

"Sure, let us. I think I'm here for two reasons, which do you want to hear first?"

"Tell me the lie first."

"I'm here to rescue Angelica."

"Rescue?"

"Angelica."

"That's amusing."

"Angelica Alfa-Ochoa, know her?"

"In a sense. I know who you think she was. The other reason?"

"I'm looking for Exeter Mondragon. That's you, isn't it?"

This seems to have the force of novelty if nothing else.

"Think of the special status of the man, such as yourself, condemned to imminent death. What's his greatest gift? Simple, the gift of knowledge. Sometimes even wisdom. Here's what I mean. You ask me if I am Exeter Mondragon. Your breath even catches as you say the name.

"Now, this kind of question, asking someone to confirm their identity, is fundamentally benign and asked maybe a billion times a day across this globe. But it's almost never asked of me. The kind of words the speaker intuits may be their last.

"This is where your special status comes in. Because at this precise moment I am, in essence, speaking to a ghost. And no one cares what ghosts know because of their inability to *do*. So, yes, ghost, I am Exeter Mondragon."

We sit there in silence.

But not really silence because now it seems all those elements we are told exist in the universe but do so invisibly so that we have to take their existence on faith, the quarks and neutrinos and superstrings and the rest of God's particles, all of them are emitting a low dissonant hum that is either growing in intensity or else becoming the only thing I can attend to. I need to create any competing sound.

"Don't you want to know who I am?" I say.

"The way you phrase that is interesting."

"I try."

"It interests because it implies a kind of quid pro quo. In other words, you now know who I am, don't I therefore desire reciprocity?"

"Don't you?"

"I told you my name, even told you why I told you it. Among the most zealously guarded information in the world, that's true, but at its core still just a name. Do you feel you know me as a result?"

"I know your handiwork, had to walk through it to get here."

"Because if names are dispositive of the question, I already know who you are. Agree, Riv del Rio?"

"I don't think I know you because you confirmed your name, I know you because you're very knowable. And in the most uninteresting way possible."

"Oh. Let's test that, then. See, I must be less arrogant than you. Because I don't believe I know you, Riv. Not in the sense of the word we've been using.

"And I say that despite the following being true. I know every discernible fact there is to know about you. I know, down to the penny, the amount of money you've earned and spent in your life and I know that the latter far exceeds the former. I know every address, phone number, medical condition you've ever had. I not only know your date of birth, I know you kept your mother in labor for eighteen hours. And I hope you like symmetry because I now know the exact date of your death and further know that, in a nice bit of it, I am going to make your death last eighteen hours as well.

"I know all that yet still wouldn't presume to say that I know you in any meaningful way. But I will. I will know you. That's the difference between us. You will die, soon, knowing nothing more about me than you do now. While you are about to lay bare all that you are as a human, with me as your audience."

"Seems unlikely."

"You will forgive me if I don't credit you much as an evaluator of likelihoods. For example, what did you think was likely to happen when you walked in here, alone and unarmed?"

"Didn't give it much thought."

"Clearly. And now it's too late to think of anything else."

"I told you why I'm here, and it wasn't about likelihoods."

"We will get to that, I promise. First, let me explain about this great intimacy that is going to pass between us. Along with the reasons I am so confident that at its conclusion I will know you better even than you know yourself to this point, sitting across from me in gross uncertainty.

"You see, to best assess someone you have to experience them *in extremis*, and the ultimate extremity one can deploy is imminent death. Let me amend that a bit. The truly ultimate extremity is the prolonged consciousness of an externally volitional imminent death paired with a special kind of physical suffering. I am well-versed in death, of course. But I am a peerless expert in this particular species of that genus.

"It's a highly intentional expertise. I long ago decided that just snapping my fingers to end a life was, more than anything, a missed opportunity."

"More than anything? I can think of a great many more accurate ways to characterize those acts."

"Careful, Riv. I'm enjoying humouring you for the moment, indeed. But I'm not so tied to my methodology that I won't just snap my fingers again. What's saving you for now is your unadulterated powerlessness."

He focuses on me and I try to match his stare. I cannot. Behind those eyes I see centuries. Centuries of malice and hatred and lies. The reason I can't begin to place how old he is is that he is all ages at once. Eternal not just in spirit and scope but in adaptations. I look away.

"Look at me when I'm talking to you, Riv. I can't imagine you want to be rude. So, as I was saying, what I do is, when there's someone who is about to die."

"You mean someone you've decided to kill."

"If you prefer. Is I take someone for whom that's true and I start by establishing conclusively to them that their death is both certain and imminent. That's critical. There can be no hope of a reprieve. Then I add the element of physical suffering. Not just any old kind of physical suffering, of course. Profound, deep, extravagant physical suffering to which I attach the kind of medical and biological intervention that's designed to prolong and enhance the suffering at every turn. Lastly, I confess, I'm a sucker for metaphor. Every artist needs it and I'm no exception. I try to suit the punishment to the crime and if there's no crime to punish then to the supple demands of irony."

"No crime to punish?"

"Correct. Death sentences can be earned a variety of ways in my world. You actively cross me, that's an obvious one. Or maybe your simple existence is an impediment to the advancement of my many hidden interests, there's another. But I also find that it's important to occasionally include the random innocent, difficult as they may sometimes be to find."

"Like Angelica?"

He laughs. "No, not alike."

"Why include innocents at all?"

"I told you. The old way was a missed opportunity. Opportunities to learn. About humanity under extremest duress. About death, despair, the soul. The old ways, like flipping a light off with a switch, offered none of that. So instead, artistry.

"Did you talk too much and to the wrong listeners? Maybe your tongue is removed and the remainder of your body scalpeled down until you resemble nothing more than a giant tongue.

"Or maybe you'll die having made manifest the circular reasoning you were prone to, an element that made your life like the revolution of a giant wheel with no discernible peaks and valleys or advancements, just rote repetitions and returns."

"Ah."

"As for the innocents, no competent study of human despair could succeed without them. People severely underestimate the outsized role a certain feeling in the sufferer plays in making their suffering worse. The best way I can describe this feeling is that it is very much like what's commonly called *feeling sorry for yourself*. I am saying that a significant and exacerbating element of suffering is the person's meta-understanding that they are suffering.

"Picture yourself being physically and mentally tortured, soon you won't have to merely imagine it, and project the kinds of thoughts that might provide comfort. You might, for example, say to yourself that your suffering is unavoidable or temporary, common tactics. But you might also voice a very strange consolation. That one appeals to a kind of invented moral arbiter of the universe and wonders if the suffering isn't deserved.

"Why does that work? Because the reality is it *does* work, at least somewhat. By the by, this all aligns nicely with a strong area of interest for me. Why does the liar feel a kind of autonomic compunction during the act? And what is being appealed to when we speak of this *deserving* as it relates to suffering?

"None of that is germane anyway since, as I'm saying, I remove all potential forms of succor. In the case of the innocent participant—"

"Victim."

"—they know full well that there is nothing unavoidable about what is happening to them. I make it abundantly clear that this is not just something that is happening to them. No, this is something I am *doing* to them and doing so basically on a whim. That their suffering is not temporary but rather final. And they know, as well as they've ever known anything, that they don't *deserve* what's happening to them, whatever that means. It's really this randomness of it all, I think, that makes the recipient feel like they have been orphaned from life. That's how easy it is to strip their universe of all meaning."

"Yes, one part limitless resources, many parts epically-diseased mind."

"Understand that I don't alter basal facts. I don't distort, I reveal. The emptiness and the entropy. And if it's consolation you seek, you're in the wrong neighborhood. You want your death served up by natural causes, I make your end as unnatural as possible in a way that makes you question nature itself. You try to console yourself that your loved one must not have suffered much at the end, ask yourself why the *did he suffer much* question is so popular, but I send one of my buttons to your home to disabuse you of that notion and inform you that, yes, your loved one suffered an inconceivable amount and for an inconceivable duration."

I process this last detail and I swear it's what knocks my heart back out of time. I should have died long ago of this mistempo. Or for that matter pick literally any other cause of death and it would still be preferable to this reality. Better yet, I should've outlasted everyone of personal significance, the way I outlasted Jane, so that I could now die in peace without any concern for collateral damage.

I'm looking around for anything I can use but see only myself looking around for anything I can use. I remember that I am sitting on a stool and that a stool to the head can't feel good. But he is shaking a smile side to side as I realize the stool is bolted to the floor and further realize it's just as well, as it would've probably only made him angry.

"Now let's talk about you," he says. "In your case I certainly cannot even entertain the notion of having an innocent on my hands. Still, I always prefer it when a person, necessarily a deeply deluded person, comes to me as a perceived exercise of their waning liberty. Even if the reality is that they are more like heavy spheres released from atop the Tower of Pisa *deciding* to hit the ground below."

"You know why I'm here."

"I do. But, more importantly, in the next eighteen hours I'm going to ensure that you see the reason you are here. I mean that *see* literally too. Because ultimately yours was a failure of vision. You thought you saw an orderly world. One with rules and established recipes that lead to positive results. You thought you saw these things, but they weren't actual.

"While other things you failed to see entirely. How flesh doesn't penetrate brick walls. How you don't start clearing a jungle unless you're prepared to become one of its beasts. Mostly you did not see how the interconnection of All is one of those concepts that sounds good on paper but in reality spells desolation.

"What explains this kind of hallucinatory blindness? A person sees what they directly look at and struggles to see anything else. You have not often enough cast your gaze on the world at large. You prefer to look at yourself. So I'm going to give you what you most crave.

"In a short while a doctor is going to come in here to run an A-line from your groin. Well, he's not really a doctor, he's a butcher, but butchers and doctors wear similar coats and serve similar purposes. We will be using this line to slowly empty you of the approximately five litres of blood you currently contain and timing it so that you die precisely eighteen hours from now. Another way of looking at it is that the emptiness of all that *is* will be invading your very core.

"I know what you are thinking. What will I be seeing during this process? No mystery. I told you that this is the last room you will ever be in and we know that the only thing for you to see in this room, once I leave, is you.

"Here is the problem with that *for* you. Have you ever stared at your mirror image for an unnaturally long time? Probably not, and a clear majority of those who *have* would never willingly repeat the experience. It is deeply unpleasant. People see apparitions. They watch their own faces distort horribly. See fantastic wretches and monsters. They see the faces of their deceased then watch those grossly distort. And note that these effects emerge in minutes, whereas your effects will be transpiring over the aforementioned eighteen hours. Also, we have already tailored the lighting and other factors in here to achieve maximal effect. I am sure you would expect nothing less.

"Now, I will not spend any of our scarce time limning the bioneural bases for these well-established phenomena. I will just add, as a matter of responsible disclosure, that I have described only the physical manifestations of this process. But we know that purely physical explanations miss so much and only fully satisfy the fundamentally uncurious. Scientists constantly rush together, like grade school children with a charged secret, and pursue the same goal. To drain the mystery out of life.

"They fail and always will fail. So let me just say this about your upcoming eighteen hours. As interesting as these physical effects are, they pale next to the psychological and even philosophical trial you are about to endure."

"Is this how you killed Angelica?"

"Oh, you know better than to sneak in that momentous of an implied premise."

"Except truth is a complete defense and I know you killed her."

"You *know*? Truly people throw that word around too loosely, pet peeve of mine. Here is how loose you are being, Angelica is alive."

"And well?"

"That's trickier, of course."

"Take me to her, then."

"Then what?"

"Then I'll know you're telling the truth and in the future I'll be far more circumspect about using the word *know*."

"First, you have no future. And even if you did, we run things around here as a dictatorial meritocracy. Given that, you have done nothing to merit something as grand as learning the fate of Angelica."

"Only I'm not here to learn her fate, I'm here to change it."

"No, see, I used the word *fate* very purposefully. *Fate* as in not subject to change. What is fated to happen to someone is fixed and unfixable, never more true than in the case of Angelica."

"Save that fate nonsense for teens. No such thing. In this world you get people and their acts. If something happens to Angelica it'll be because you did it and I failed to stop you, not because of some invented mythical entity."

"How does one person manage to be so consistently wrong? The element we call fate, where human action and decision-making is of no moment, everything encompassed by that term, undoubtedly exists. The reason you are able to fool yourself into thinking it doesn't is that you never see it naked and whenever confronted with its effects those effects are always attributable to mundane factors like choice. But today is your lucky day, may not feel that way, because today you absolutely can see fate. Just stop looking at yourself in the mirror and look into my eyes. I am fate.

"I am what you are all unwittingly thinking of when you use that word. The reason human activity is powerless in the face of the predetermined. An entity with complete and total control and you are locking eyes with it at this very moment.

"Contrast this with a similar situation, a popular and enduring countervailing metaphor. Those who intelligently use the word *God* use it to subsume a whole host of concepts and phenomena. But while those effects may exist, the reality is they have no antecedent cause. God does not exist. It may have at some point, and the word can still be a useful referent, but God is dead. This is not opinion, it is fact. I know this because it has been my life's work. To reach the point where I can say this with perfect clarity and sobriety. I killed God."

Was that some kind of cue? Because in walks the presumed doctor or butcher or doctor, and he is pushing on wheels a set of either medical or butchering implements. He is immediately horrifying in every way it is possible to be horrifying.

I go to stand, nothing more than a visceral reaction really, and know immediately that standing is not going to happen. A vicious jolt runs up and through my system and I am forcefully glued to the stool as if it were a limbic part of me. I try again but find I can no longer command my lower half.

Now my pants are coming off and the butcher is sticking a needle in my upper inner thigh. My heart slows, maybe back to the correct beat. Next he's up around my shirt.

"I told you I was going to get to truly know you. That's just a microphone so that I won't miss a syllable of what you say in the next eighteen hours."

"I'm not going to say anything."

"You think that, but listen to experience, you will. And because I predict you will prove both voluble and valuable, I am quite looking forward to the content. Can you think of a better way to exercise one's authority?"

"You have no legitimate authority, only perversion."

"No authority? Have you not been listening? I am Fate, and the killer of God to boot. What higher authority are you looking for? And note the critical fact that I don't state those things the way people might say they have red hair or you specifically might say you have green eyes, very attractive ones, I concede.

"No, I state those things as a way of listing accomplishments. These are things I *did*, not accidents of birth. I grew up sifting through dumpsters for sustenance and today even the wind answers to me. So, yes, I claim, literally, the highest authority there is. The one I forcefully wrested from the universe and placed in my lap like a pet."

"You're so untouchable, beyond any of our reaches. Unlike us mere mortals, you need not concern yourself with conventional nuisances like blame and admissions of guilt. Why not write a letter to Angelica's mother detailing her daughter's innocence and explaining what happened to her? She shouldn't go on thinking her daughter killed herself. She should know the truth. Likewise—"

"Should, shouldn't, I warned you this is an area of interest. You say this woman shouldn't labor under a painful lie. I say why not? Help me out here. Who or what, besides you, says she should not?"

"Anyone of sound mind and soul would agree."

"So you say I am unsound and I counter sound. Hmm, how can we break this tie? I know, let's let the universe decide. Whoever lives longer wins. Deal?"

"No deal."

"Anyway, you were about to make another request, I believe."

I am in all sorts and facets of pain and disorientation and I can't quite remember my reasoning so I just default to my original position.

"Nothing further," I say.

"Your hesitation is unnecessary. You can mention them without disclosing anything or increasing any danger they face."

"My cousins."

"Ah, yes. Fernando and Mauricio del Rio."

"They're safe?"

"I didn't say that. I said nothing you say can increase their peril. The flipside, of course, is that nothing you say or do can decrease it either. Starting to get the picture now about your powerlessness?"

"So their peril is a fluid element. Meaning they're alive?"

"Very good, yes. Your cousins remain alive."

"Let them go. They know nothing. And even if they did, they are like me, powerless to hurt you or your interests in any way. They're only even involved because of my moral carelessness. They respect your authority."

He is laughing but like no laughter ever before sounded.

"This last appeal of yours is the most humourous yet. It amounts to you asking me to release your cousins in order to allay your feelings of guilt during these last eighteen hours. Does that fit my profile? I have told you that I exist to deepen despair, misery, horror. But despite that I'm going to release your cousins? Why? Because you asked nicely?"

"Just an opportunity, then."

"Meaning?"

"Meaning you have a belief system. You should be looking for any high-value opportunities to test it and thereby acquire valuable confirmations."

"My belief is that you will soon die after experiencing the most excruciating eighteen hours of your equal parts miserable and meaningless life. The confirmation, when it comes, will add nothing to my understanding of our world."

"Exactly, because of the predictability. That's why you need me, to introduce the element of chance. What I call chance, anyway. You would call it a misperception."

"How do you propose to do that?"

"Let's you and I engage in a contest. Not a physical one, at the moment it's taking all my remaining strength just to form these words. A mental one. We can contest each other over a chess board. One game. If you win or we draw, you can do with me as you wish. But if I win all you have to do is release four people unharmed. Four meaningless people, you would say, with no ability to hurt you in any manner."

"Three meaningless. Angelica is rife with meaning."

"You can play white."

"I just love negotiating with someone who has nothing to give, nothing to offer, and because they've already lost everything, nothing to lose."

"But isn't it you who has nothing to lose? You've made it abundantly clear that there is no way I survive this. So the second you agree to my terms I must then necessarily lose our game."

"Decent attempt, kudos, but remember that I know all facts that pertain to you. So, no."

"Poker, then."

"Same answer."

"You're missing the point. The more I'm expected to win, the higher quality the confirmation of your worldview when I lose, no?"

"I appreciate your concern, but I am in no need of confirmations. So you will not be playing Bergmanesque chess with Death, sorry. You'll just be rolling over for it like everybody else. But first look at this."

He holds something up between his fingers. I can't make out what it is, just that it is moving. He stands and walks it over to me with care.

Now his butcher is installing a brace of sorts around my neck so that I can only stare straight ahead. Then he's attaching strange translucent glasses to my face that prevent my eyelids from shutting. Tears march down my face.

"Don't mind that," Mondragon says. "We have to overstimulate your tear ducts so that your eyes can remain continuously open without drying out. Wouldn't want you to miss any of the sights. Look at this, for example."

Before me is an inverted cockroach suspended from one of its legs by Mondragon. It wriggles furiously, but none of that changes its position meaningfully. I think of Woolf's moth, then realize I probably deserve to die for thinking of something like that at a moment like this.

"Really look at it, though," Mondragon adds. "We call someone an *insect* to insult them, yes? But look closely at this creature. Would you say it is suffering right now as it struggles to free itself from my control? You might say yes but also say that it has a limited capacity for suffering. Just as it has a limited capacity for joy or even plain satisfaction. But I tell you now that, in this instant, this creature is superior to you in every way. It suffers less and, lacking the concepts of joy and satisfaction, mourns the absence of nothing.

"Very soon it will have more than you as well. See the spasmodic jerking? That is life. There's no word that better sums up what every one of these single kicks represents and what you, who can no longer kick, are losing apace.

"To be lower than a cockroach because the cockroach exceeds you in the only element that matters. You who once ran and hoped and created but now only pray and lament and will soon be incapable of even that."

186 · SERGIO DE LA PAVA

He lets it drop and it scurries away gratefully as I fill with confirmatory envy.

"Soon any neutral observer looking down from above will judge our friend there of greater dignity than you, a decomposing collection of bones that feeds the soil insects scavenge from."

He vanishes.

I am alone in the room. I can move my head only slightly, the rest of my body not at all, eyes forced open.

My reflection is still just my reflection. It reflects the gradual loss of the half century of lifeblood I'd managed to store, a loss I'm already starting to feel. Reflects the bad decisions and hubris that put me on this stool. Reflections of and on a misspent life now devolving into an inglorious death.

Now I'm starting to see what Mondragon was talking about. At first, I attributed the sudden strangeness of my own face to the novelty of this situation. But novelty can't explain my face starting to melt like ice cream in the sun. While somehow the most pronounced features of my heavily pronounced face grow even more pronounced. I will not speak.

I start to feel better when I realize it's not my face at all I'm staring at. I don't recognize it. I so don't recognize it that I'm not only sure it is not my face, I'm pretty sure I never really had a face. That my belief to the contrary all these years was an illusion. One that was somehow both powerful enough that I never doubted it even slightly yet also evanescent enough that it could disappear in seconds, leaving no trace to argue for its previous existence. I am dumb.

Not having a face is one thing, not having existed quite another. The contingency of my existence I have always easily and sanely accepted. That I will soon cease to exist has been recently hammered home to me quite effectively and I had taken tentative steps toward acceptance. Even a claim that I don't currently exist is potentially open to acceptance. But that I have never existed except within a delusion, that no one can ever prove otherwise, everything all along a simulation for the benefit of one person and that person doesn't even exist, that possibility then realization is now becoming perfectly debilitating.

At the worst time too because now I am seeing the dead and watching them die what seem like further deaths whose main purpose is to take them from human to animal to monster. My father and Jane and people I'd forgotten had died or, even now, am not entirely sure have died. I remain dumb.

Not sure they were ever alive but Mondragon has dead eyes. Two black orbs of coal that are growing past the point his face can accommodate. Impossible that they can even absorb the necessary light to create vision.

"Bring him back into coherence now," the face with the eyes says. Then, "Do you and I have a different definition of that word? *Now*, as in right *now* your very existence depends on your ability to get this man to understand what I am about to say to him."

The lights are back on. The eyeglasses off. I can close my eyes again and I do. But the perfect dark scares me so I reopen them. Mondragon and his butcher are staring at me and the mirrors are either gone or I am in a different room.

"There's been a significant change in plans," says Mondragon, looking distracted and maybe annoyed. "The upshot is we are leaving here for our next step. Nothing pedestrian drives us, of course. You may as well try to verbally coax a caterpillar into more quickly digesting itself inside its chrysalis. But the step is no less necessary and before I ascend it I would like to try to cram eighteen hours of entertainment into the next few minutes."

The butcher is preparing an injection. He has the kind of smile that just makes everything worse.

"Are you with us, Riv? Because you are going to be making a decision here."

"I'm here."

"Completely?"

"Physically."

"See that's the problem, because you will think it's a rather critical decision. We will proceed regardless. First, the potential windfall. You are free to leave. I am not going to lie to you, it will not be the most dignified exit. You will be discarded like trash. Stripped of all your clothes. Your head and entire body shaved. You will be placed in a van, within a large vat of amniotic fluid, driven out to the Cali River in the centre of town, and very loudly and unceremoniously dumped there. You will suffer no more physical harm than that."

"But. If."

"Neither applies, I have laid out all the pertinent details."

"Bizarre details, you forgot bizarre."

"No, context is all. The details are intentional and, above all, apt. You are, in all but a minor sense, a dead man. One who wants life. But you cannot have life without a preceding birth, can you? If I grant you life, if you choose this, you must be born into that life. Birth signifies coming into this proving ground wearing only afterbirth on your hairless skin, your bald pate full of nothing useful, and your cries imbued with the unmistakable plaint of impotence."

"My cousins and Angelica in the van too?"

"How would you know? Do you ask infants questions? It's not for you, as a helpless babe, to have this information. Just enjoy your freedom and the special knowledge that you are among the extremely select few to have survived even a mildly pointed interaction with me. These questions you have, on those questions your tabula will remain as rasa as a newborn's."

I'm trying and failing to remember exactly how Fercho and Mauro came to be involved in this hot mess to begin with. I doubt

I had anything to do with it but I'm also perfectly certain I am entirely responsible.

"Don't look so glum, pal. You are such a big fan of choice and chance, those twin authors of so much human agony, that I am going to graciously give you both. More accurately, I am going to offer you both, an opportunity to further demonstrate your admiration. Because you can choose another course. And that course has a significant element of chance attached.

"Look at Dr. Carnicero's right hand. Exercise this second option and he will inject you with that syringe he's holding. The syringe was picked at random by the good doctor from among an unlabeled pile of them. Neither he nor I know its precise contents. We know it is one of two substances and that the chance of it being either is fifty percent.

"So the syringe may contain potassium chloride. This would be very bad news for your heart, a real showstopper. Or the syringe may contain midazolam. This would actually be rather pleasant for you, a very deep sleep with no long-term adverse physical consequences. I am operating under some time constraints here, which will it be?"

"Why would I ever choose this second option with its fifty percent chance of killing me?"

"Oh, right, forgot. If you pick this second option I will release your cousins."

"They're alive?"

"I told you they live, are you calling me a liar?"

"What about Angelica?"

"Also alive. You enjoy repetition this much?"

"No, what happens to her if I take the injection?"

"What happens or doesn't happen to Angelica is as preordained as ordinations come. I will say this, however. If you take the injection and, more importantly, survive it, I will take you to Angelica. All your Angelica-related queries will be answered. You may not like those answers, but you will get them. And if you want to continue deluding yourself that you can effect change, I will not interfere in your belief. You can learn the truth organically."

I swear to God I understood maybe half of what he'd said. I picture myself explaining my continuing life to interested others. I wonder aloud if I can get some of my blood back.

"Your decision, Riv. Decide or I will, and that rarely works out well for people in your position."

"Hurry up and give me the shot before I change my mind."

"Is that right? Are you certain you understood the full parameters?"

"I understood, hurry."

"My, look who pretends to give orders suddenly. Right, well, every man should steer his own ship, even if it is directly into the rocks. Please proceed, Carnicero, grant the man his wish. Good chance it will be the last one he ever sees fulfilled."

I watch the needle go in.

"This, Riv, is, I admit, genuine suspense."

The little plunger pushes the liquid into me.

"The colour is no clue, both are yellow."

I don't feel anything. But that's probably what death is.

"I find myself rooting for you, Riv del Rio. So few of this world's inhabitants ever surprise me anymore. Your decision just now managed it."

I give some thought to my last words. What are the greatest, because toughest, last words ever uttered? Because that's what I'm going for. I look straight into Mondragon's dead eyes.

"Blurft," I say.

"Save your strength," he says. "In the unlikely event there's another side, you'll need it there."

The world is everything that exists and nothing that doesn't.

"In the meantime," Mondragon says. "Close your eyes and count to death."

A SABBATH OF WITCHES

The history of sainthood as distinguishable from a history of saints. Only God can create a saint. Only man, steeped in the ways of the Catholic Church, can confirm the creation. And withal the path to sainthood may be arduous and long, it is also open to great variation, perhaps reflecting the nigh-infinite ways moral lives can differ.

In the beginning, the process was stable and simple. The first saints were martyrs. Brave souls who died for their faith at the hands of Roman rule and in the immediate shadow of Jesus's death. Their canonization more the product of mere formality than any earthly deliberation.

The ensuing centuries saw a relaxation of that mortal standard. To be sure, martyrdom remained a proper and powerful method for entry into the sanctum. Yet it is known that inclusivity does not necessarily indicate exclusivity, and the category of Saint grew to encompass those who had not paid the ultimate price but who nonetheless, on the scaffolding of their great faith, had in their lives and actions displayed a great piety redolent of perfection. The category grew like an exponent.

Around the year 1200, Pope Alexander III, concerned that the standard had become too relaxed, and offended by one particular example, took action in the form of a decree. He decreed through a decree that it was thereby decreed that going forward only the Pope had the power to declare someone a saint.

192 · SERGIO DE LA PAVA

Four centuries later came greater formalization. Candidates who were not martyrs were subject to a strict requirement. They must have performed a minimum of four posthumous miracles before achieving sainthood. The determination remained the Pope's to make.

The two-step determination was a rigorous one. First came beatification, a papal recognition that a particular candidate was worthy of consideration. At this stage the church would assign a so-called Devil's Advocate whose task was to argue against sainthood. Only those who overcame the diabolical arguments graduated to step two, canonization. Canonization, formal recognition by the Pope that the person at issue is in fact a saint, is not the creation of a new reality, it is human recognition of a divine truth.

Today, canonization remains a two-step process, but a less rigorous one that makes concessions to modernity. Devil's Advocates are no longer employed and the requisite miracles have been halved from four to two. The result is that over the last half century more saints have been canonized than in the entire previous history of saints being canonized. Whether this lessening of standards speaks of something integral to our times is left for the reader to determine.

What follows is not a comprehensive history of all the saints or even of a portion of the saints. It is a brief précis of one extraordinary saint. A saint whose life exemplifies the dichotomy we live daily as prisoners of the moral universe. The saint who lends his name to this very land.

Saint Cyprian of Carthage was born circa 200 AD. He led an exemplary life. He was a highly educated and wealthy man who, following his conversion, gave liberally to the poor and, as bishop, presided over very tumultuous times before, in the ultimate, dying a martyr's death at the hands of the Romans. This writing is not about him.

This is about an altogether different saint who shares his

name. This has led to some confusion. Not helped by the thoroughly enigmatic nature of this second saint. No, this is about "The Magician" Saint Cyprian.

Saint Cyprian of Antioch was born in the third century AD. in ancient Greece and under the goddess Aphrodite, whose birthplace he was named after. His family was steeped in magic and pagan sorcery, so he received extensive training in these black arts. By early adulthood he was expert in astrology, numerology, supernatural spells, and, most especially, expert in conjuring and communing with demons.

At age thirty, Cyprian entombed himself in a cave in order to better commune with the demonic underworld that he might deepen his diabolical skills and understanding even further. There, by employing a variety of nefarious rituals and sacrifices, he made intimate contact with the Malignant One himself. The Deceiver dictated to him, in the language of the spectral world, agonized moans and shrieks, his grimoire, or book of magic spells.

Cyprian was now a supreme conduit between our ordinary world and the netherworld. And his Book of Saint Cyprian survives to this day, albeit along with continuing disputes about its authorship and whether the book is actually not a cohesive single-source whole but rather an amalgam of several grimoires spanning centuries and written more than a millennium after Cyprian's death. Never in dispute again was his expertise in malicious wizardry.

As news of Cyprian's otherworldly skills spread, so too did appeals for his sorcerous interventions. In one pivotal instance, he was approached by a young man by the name of Gladio, who entreated his assistance in a vital courtship interpolation. The object was Justina, a remarkably beautiful virgin known for her integrity, and the would-be tool of one of Cyprian's famous supernatural love spells.

Cyprian had the spell poised at the ready to activate its sinister ministrations, but instead it was he who fell under the natural world's longest-running spell: romantic love. At first sight of Justina, Cyprian decided that his spell would actually be directing the love of this great beauty toward *him*, not the undeserving Gladio.

Never considered was even the notion that the eventual litany of spells directed at Justina would prove ineffective. Yet that's precisely what transpired. Cyprian taxed his occult abilities to the utmost but Justina proved impervious to fiendish manipulation.

A frustrated Cyprian sought demonic counsel to solve his predicament. The answer came from Satan himself, who informed Cyprian that Justina was that rarest commodity, a true Christian. And her Christianity was so powerful that there was no utility in seeking novel charms or spells or refining existing ones. The Fallen Angel's intent was to dissuade further attempts by Cyprian that might redound into a loss of prestige for the infernal arts.

Convinced that Cyprian was too spellbound to abandon his quest, the Tempter increased his direct involvement. He approached Justina himself with three of his best devils. Each devil succeeded his predecessor with a different powerful spell. But each time, Justina, who was immersed at the time in one of her frequent devotional intervals of prayer and fasting, could sense the supernatural attack on her virtue. And each time she successfully parried the attack through more intense prayer and, when most vulnerable, by making the sign of the cross while gripping her most prized crucifix.

Cyprian witnessed Justina successfully repel the Deceiver and his physical attraction deepened into multifaceted love. He understood that Justina's beauty spanned over more than just the tangible and he pondered over its source. He had his own travail before him in ridding himself of the Accuser's grip. He chose emulation. He burned his books on astrology and magic and in place studied deeply the teachings of Christ. He embraced the passion of the convert and, most crucially, made timely applications of the sign of the cross while holding a meaningful crucifix. Not only was he liberated from the satanic grip, he won the love of Justina in the process.

Together, Saint Cyprian and Saint Justina led powerfully Christian lives. Cyprian ultimately became a bishop and Justina the abbess of a convent. In word and deed they tirelessly spread Christ's message of selfless love.

In 304 AD, at the behest of the Roman emperor Diocletian, they were seized and taken to Damascus to be tortured. There Cyprian was torn apart piece by piece using red-hot pincers and Justina harmed in ways the universe cannot bear to attach words to. When Cyprian was placed in boiling-hot water but did not burn, the judge decreed that the emperor himself should decide their fate.

Brought before Emperor Diocletian at Nicomedia, Cyprian and Justina were asked a simple question. Would they renounce their faith in a sole Christian God and pledge fealty instead to the Roman plurality of gods? They would not. They were beheaded on the banks of the River Gallus and their bodies denied burial.

The legacy of Saint Cyprian is a complicated one. Even the moderately skilled armchair theologian will raise questions. In the end, Cyprian won the love of Justina. So can we say with certainty that the diabolical methodology indeed failed? Also, what was it about Cyprian's nature that allowed him to achieve such lofty stature in the dark world? Was his a genuine conversion or just a cynical ploy to win the affections of Justina? Why didn't he boil to death in the water? Couldn't someone as talented as Cyprian essentially perform Christianity without genuine Christian feeling? Is there any meaning or import to such a distinction?

His eponymous San Cipriano, Colombia, is no less complicated. There's a reason it's not called San Justina. A tiny village of maybe five hundred inhabitants located a stone's throw from the port city of Buenaventura, it is literally inaccessible by any means other than witchcraft. Visitors to this mysterious location are transported via a little witch, or *brujita*, a centaur-like combination of motorcycle and giant wooden crate, that operates on railroad tracks long ago fallen into disuse.

In conclusion, while allocating the proper measures between cause and effect can be challenging, San Cipriano is a place that so creates its own special and isolated reality that one quickly comes to believe it could only have been named after The Magician.

"He's waking up."

"No, he's not."

"Oh, no? Look at his eyes. What do you call that?

"You, you waking up?"

These guys talking. About me, at me, around me. My eyes are open and it feels like a mistake, the kind cannot be undone.

On my right is a motorcycle somehow. It is attached to and propelling the crate I am on and at the helm is I guess a woman. Here eyeballs are purely white, so she's blind. She is operating a motorcycle and she cannot see. She cannot see, but it's not a problem because we are somehow linked to railroad tracks. No turns possible, just a one-way descent.

She is taking us deeper and deeper into a jungle and two men are staring intently at my face and none of it makes any sense at all, or maybe everything external to me makes perfect sense while I personally make none.

I can't move, can't talk, but my mental clarity may be rising. Going deeper and deeper into a jungle like this, how is it that I am being forcibly taken further and further into a jungle's depths like this?

There's a strange sound. The four of us exerting pressure onto the tracks is creating a harsh screech.

But it isn't. The sound is coming from the motorcycle. No, from its operator.

This woman is dying. I mean that, looking at her, the primary impression she gives off is of death relentlessly encroaching on life. I think her back is broken, one of her arms too. Her hair is like ash, her skin a collection of sores. On the bridge of her nose, I painfully discover, is a vile growth that serves as replica in miniature of her corpse in full.

Her mouth. It's open and I suddenly understand that the dissonant sound is coming from there. And her breath is visible. Against all sense it is visible, because it's not cold enough for that. Not cold at all. We're in a damned swamp being roasted alive and her breath is visible when she makes this unfathomable sound.

The sound itself. Its disturbing timbre. I can't place its nature. What is this wretched noise? Is it like the light from stars that no longer exist? The present as pure testimony about the past. Like this sound, vestigial, testifying to the existence of a painful world long ago replaced by one no better in any respect. Yes.

So my surprise when all that remained true, but a more direct companion truth also emerged. This creature is laughing. Laughter. And not sardonic or forced. This is unmistakably the laughter that can only flow from pleasure. Everything about everything is wrong as can be, but to this laugher the apt response to that fact is pure delight.

The other two start talking to each other and I see why. Ahead of us, on the same tracks but pointed our way and fast approaching, is a contraption equal to ours but with much more humanity on board.

Our motorcyclist slows down not at all, laughs even louder, until a hard brake when passage becomes impossible. It's a standoff between us and their side, which appears to consist of two tourist families and the two locals they are paying to be part of their game of pretend. I decide they're either German or Babylonian.

Their local speaks first. You know the rule, he says. The *brujita* with less cargo gets off the track so the other can pass. You appear to be transporting one individual, he adds, we are moving seven. He awaits a response, then appears to see our driver for the first time and visibly recoils.

My two guys look at each other and smile. Our creature laughs. This other *brujita* is appropriately unsettled by this sound.

The one guy, the one who was sure I was waking up, is listening to their restatement of the rule and nodding along. But he's saying nothing, just that smile. Now he's rubbing his chin, but in a performative way that seems designed to display the back of his right hand.

Whatever's on there, his audience sees it and it changes everything. Now the two locals are frantically ordering everyone off the *brujita* and dragging it off the tracks. Everyone understands that the rules of man are subject to erasure. Everyone but one.

One of the tourists is using some of the most broken Spanish I have ever heard to complain at large. He doesn't understand why established procedure isn't being followed. That and fundamental fairness, he seems to be invoking. That he doesn't understand is obvious. It's the true depths of his failure to understand that he can't possibly comprehend.

Because he still hasn't said a word, but the man who displayed the back of his hand has almost magically acquired a very large machete and is walking toward the complainer's group. Maybe there are multiple ways to interpret this act, but not for the two locals, they turn and run into the jungle. The tourists see this and start screaming and crying. The creature laughs and this increases the tourists' screaming and crying. They also run away, leaving a trail of diminuendoing lament.

Only the talking man remains, and he is still talking. He says he's not looking for trouble. Like that has anything to do with anything.

I wonder if this might not be a good time to attempt an escape. Then I remember I am here pursuant to some kind of agreement. That and I am not entirely sure I can even move my legs.

The talking finally stops because the tourist cannot talk because he cannot breathe because Mondragon's man has his hand around his neck. He drives the tourist neckfirst onto his back, uses his foot to pin the man's arm to the ground at the wrist, then drives his machete through the palm and into the earth like he's staking a tent. The scream is guttural and epic, but the creature to my side just increases the pitch of her laugh so that the two frequencies cancel each other out.

He lets go of the machete, wipes the tourist's blood off his lips, then realizes he is missing a necessary tool so heads back to our *brujita*. The tourist is left alone, but if he wishes to run, he must first tear his hand in half. He just lies there instead, writhing and decrying the Fates. When his tormentor gets to us, he asks his partner where the bone saw is.

"Strange," I say.

"Oh, the crying woke you up?"

"Who told you you could talk?"

"Human cries wake him up, he must be the sensitive type."

"The shape of his eyes," I say. "He kind of look likes Mondragon, right?"

"What?"

"You don't agree? What about you?"

"Shut up."

"I see, neither of you has ever actually seen him."

"What's your point?"

"No point, just noting a similarity. I noticed the uncommon shape of Exeter Mondragon's eyes when he and I entered into our agreement. You must be aware of our agreement, no? It's the reason you're taking me where you're taking me, the primary aspect of our agreement and the clearest indication of

Mondragon's wishes. Well, that and the fact that time was of the essence. I remember him stating that more than once. But don't worry. If we're late, I'll explain the delay to him, exactly as it transpired."

"To explain something you need to be alive."

He has found the bone saw and is enjoying displaying its teeth to me.

"Man, that's your answer to everything." This other guy isn't as dense. "When you find yourself in a hole, first stop digging. Our instructions were clear. You want to improvise? Not with me you don't. Look where improvisation got Eladio recently."

This last comment generates the most laughter yet from the creature. I wish people would stop amusing it so much.

I see now what's on the back of their right hands and it reminds me of something. Dead skin raised by hot iron branding. An arc with a solid circle below it. Like an eye, or a giant moonbow over the globe:

No one says more, but our *brujita* restarts toward our destination, whatever that might be. I steal one last look at the tourist, the luckiest person to ever lose a hand. He appears to be in some kind of convulsive shock. Where he lies it looks as if the soil had conspired to grow unnatural flesh. As it all recedes from view, I see that the affected hand is twitching up and down.

I try to resist this thought, I do, I swear. But it looks like he is waving us goodbye.

It's a beautiful world. There's a waterfall landing in a river of emerald-green water. Giant swaying trees that will outlast us all. The kind of overpowering pulchritude that seems made up.

I have nothing to say to this kind of setting anymore. These

Colombian sights still bring awe and disbelief but now they're too laced with menace. The natural world as great deception.

Colombia knows. My two captors took special pleasure in telling me they were dropping me into the Mouth of the Devil. *Charco Trompa del Diablo* is San Cipriano's worst-kept secret, mainly because its damned people are too proud of it. I alternate between staring at the waterfall and the nearby hand-carved wooden sign that looks to have been authored by the hand of a child. The child claims that:

> *La boca del diablo no carece de dientes*
> *Devora hasta el corazón de la humanidad*

And who am I to quibble? Out of the mouth of babes and sucklings and all that.

Now, the solitude of this mouth I sit in I can get behind. I was left here alone and instructed to remain in place and wait. None of my business what exactly I am waiting for, I was told. But I suspect they just didn't know.

The way I didn't know, until this precise moment, when events have stopped dominating and the only sound is the invisibly ambient wildlife, that existence itself has a rhythm section. I understand now that it has always been there. I just wasn't attuned to it. But I hear it now, a slight but persistent percussive element. It is keeping time nicely, but it also has a kind of self-perpetuating momentum. It's propulsive though faint and misleads into thinking something momentous is about to happen when, in fact, everything has already happened.

More than that, it's imaginary, this maybe clave pattern, maybe war cadence. I am providing it and it matches up with nothing actual.

That's the problem. Whatever is going to unfold next, imagination will be little help. But mine keeps firing indiscriminately.

Hearing those drums, seeing those faces from before with the mirror, and now what it would be like to be the last-ever human, exercising dominion over all other living creatures, at least until one of them got sufficiently hungry.

I am looking around imagining my first move and realizing how little I know about postapocalyptic survival. And I'm glad propagation of the species is no longer possible because I'm not sure I would. I have to shut all this out and focus on urgent reality.

Only the drums remain. Those I can't erase and they may even be getting louder. Or closer. The drums are getting closer, which means, at a minimum, they are real.

Aside from this ontological consideration, the drums getting closer does not feel like a positive development. These drums are getting aggressive. Or this was always their nature and I'm only now having that revelation.

Now there's a snake. This serpentine emissary from hell is staring right at me, but I seem to have lost my capacity for fear. I return the stare because go back to hell.

"You hearing this?" I ask.

I break eye contact because it's getting uncomfortable.

"You think it's getting louder or just closer? Both? You think it's both, don't you, snake?"

One of the many things I'm very bad at is fixing a location for the source of a sound.

A snake's eyes. Never look into them if you don't want to blacken your soul.

I stand up and walk in the direction of the drums. They get louder because closer. Their pattern is straight from the outermost cosmic reaches of all there is and it is come to San Cipriano to drive these final events and mock the notion of contingency.

The first visual disturbance I sense is the emergence of three albino wraiths dressed entirely in white. They are responsible for the drums and they serve as harbingers for a subsequent procession so anomalous and archaic that I initially lose the power of critical thought.

The hell is that thing? It can't be. I'm no less disoriented than if an immense extraterrestrial saucer had just landed.

What it is is a giant palanquin arrayed in copious gold that, depending on positioning, fires reflected sunlight in all directions and at unpredictable intervals. There are eight highly weaponized men carrying it, and all have that same arc and circle on their right hands. I have a good guess at the passenger.

This insanity pulls up to where I stand and its curtains part. Mondragon sits between two barely clad women. They are feeding him grapes and fanning him with comically large palm leaves.

"The fuck?" I say.

He didn't talk to me, or even look at me. But he did talk *about* me. I heard him instruct that I was to be transported to the other side of the waterfall. I wondered if this was a euphemism for the euphemism of getting smoked. But before I could even remember that here was one person, if any, never in need of euphemisms, I was drenched to near drowning on a raft going directly under and through that waterfall.

On the other side is a capacious lagoon. But in place of more natural splendor the whole thing has a kind of metallic feel. I wonder if maybe this is what lies on the other side of all waterfalls the world over and I just never before experienced this fact.

No one is saying anything, least of all to me. Whenever I ask what happens next, everyone near me puts a hand on their weapon. That's the kind of thing can really tamp down a person's curiosity.

Mondragon is around and everywhere, that feels palpably true. But he is not visible or audible. I try. We just stand on the edge of this body of water, waiting. Waiting but without even the minor dignity of knowing what it is we are waiting for. Because I realize then that what rankled most was not my impertinence in asking the question, it was the fact that no one knew the answer.

No one knows anything.

"Cast your eyes on a true child of fortune, everyone." Mondragon says this loud enough, and him being who he is, that everyone immediately stops to look on me with pity. He slowly comes up close while waving everyone else away. "Is that a fair description of you, Riv?"

"Depends what you mean?"

"I don't think there is any great mystery to what I mean. You are a man who was willing to stake his very life on what amounted to a flip of a coin. That you are even here to hear these words is living testament to the esteem providence must hold you in."

"Maybe. Can I wait to see how events unfold from here before agreeing or disagreeing?"

"Events? Is that what you think this is about? Even as we approach a seminal moment in humankind? I would have thought your decision to imperil your continued existence might have enlarged your vision."

"You keep saying that as if it were something I did on a whim. But I hope you haven't forgotten that there was a promised exchange involved."

"True."

"My cousins freed."

"Done."

"I just take your word for that?"

"You can have proof if you wish."

"I wish, then my audience with Angelica."

"Everything in its proper time, Riv. Would you stand under a blistering summer sun and demand the immediate appearance of winter? I keep my promises, but first look at this."

He signals and they bring over what looks like a smaller version of the palanquin he rode in on. It must be solid gold too to judge from the way its carriers are being driven down into the earth.

"What's this? A war chest?"

"This is an ark. An ark of the testimony for our times. You know of the original ark. How it contained the tablets with the Ten Commandments and emblematized the special relationship between God and his chosen people. Well, I believe I previously disclosed to you how I killed God. But that does not mean God was devoid of good ideas. His ark was one of them and I only steal from the best."

"So, your covenant with whom?"

"Very good. My covenant with the arc of the universe. My covenant with the ark I am going to board just before the world floods again. My covenant with the geometric rise and fall of man."

I look around but I am alone on this.

"Okay. Can I see Angelica now? Maybe she and I can just return to our lives. Wishing you nothing but great success in all your future endeavors, of course."

"Disappointing, truly. I can see there is no talking to you until we settle this Angelica question. So come here, I want you to look into the water. You should know that everything you see as you look around, including this body of water, is man-made. The modesty is unnecessary actually. Everything you see is Mondragon-made. Nature serves as a kind of prison for man and I don't think I need to tell you that I am no one's prisoner."

I'm looking into the water, but all I see is my reflection. This better not end up being one of those things where he tells me that all along the only Angelica was the Angelica in me.

My image is strange. At first, I can't tell how. But now I see it. I'm spinning. Very slowly. Very counterclockwise. Then faster and faster until I disappear and am replaced by a full-fledged water vortex.

Also, the color of the water is changing. Darkness is turning to light, then a brilliant silver. The vortex grows. Then morphs into something different but related. It's like a spout effect. So some fearsome leviathan must be about to emerge.

Second it pierces the surface of the water it is abundantly clear that this is not living and breathing flesh. Water rushes off its cylindrical sides in noisy cascades while the thing keeps rising and growing in dimension until there's nothing can be seen but its overwhelming silver excess bobbing menacingly there on the surface. A giant projectile pointed directly at me and knocking my heart back out of time.

"Yes. Clutching your heart that way is exactly the appropriate response to this magnificent sight."

I'm looking at that unsettling Arc and Dot again but this one seems like the progenitor.

Also, the metal leviathan has a name. Written in bloodred across its nose.

This is *Salacia 3*.

"It looks like a bullet," I say.

"It should. I'm going to fire it straight into the heart of human progress and limitation. Don't the aesthetics need to match the aspiration?"

"I don't . . ."

"You don't?"

"You aspire to?"

"What do you recommend? But first remember that everything is currently empty so I am not trying to find or locate meaning, I aim to create meaning. The world with its constant re-creation and procreation when actually creation is the sole method for ascending through the angelic orders."

"Creation of what exactly?"

"What about July 20, 1969, AD? Was that something? I'm not asking in the colloquial form of *wasn't that something?* I ask the question literally. Forget NASA, Armstrong, or really anything with a proper name. When we landed on that rock we left a plaque asserting that *here men from planet Earth first set foot upon the moon* and that *we came in peace for all mankind.* To whom was that message directed? To ourselves, of course. We had been staring at that dead orb since our birth, never able to do anything about it. That, whatever else you want to say about it, was *something*, and we did it.

"But colour me mostly unimpressed. For one, the suspense was lacking. We knew with certainty, for example, that we wouldn't be encountering any novel life-forms. Only prepubescent boys were still fantasizing about sensational creatures. We also knew, if we were being honest, that there wasn't this great font of consequential information waiting there for us.

"We are on the precipice of embarking in the polar opposite direction. People stare out onto great galactic distances not because of any powerful relevance. They do it because any dunce with a telescope can do it. But what is out there? Nothing. Go as far as you like, same result. Does it not make a great deal more sense to go inward toward the ultimate core of the one universal location we *know* contains life?

"Let us now set proverbial sail for the very seat of consciousness. And unlike Apollo, I guarantee we will encounter, and directly confront, Life. Life in the form of some of the most nightmarish creatures imaginable. We will easily surpass the greatest depth ever attained even if we have to burrow recklessly into the lowest lows of the Mariana Trench and its Challenger Deep.

"Once there, I will twist this globe's tectonic plates into a pretzel if that's what it takes to deliver my message. So, yes, a bullet. Because this kind of operation is always violent and, unlike NASA, I do not come in peace."

A kind of side hatch opens on the structure, emitting a sibilant hiss that makes me long for when a snake was my biggest problem. Equipment and people are being loaded in. Many of the people don't appear thrilled at this development as they are silently escorted in as pairs. Lots of them give off a scientist or engineer vibe.

"Can I see Angelica now?"

"What a fundamentally odd reaction to what I have just declared. But, fine. You have a one-track mind on this. Get inside and your fervent wish will at last be granted."

"Get inside this giant submarine?"

My heart had just realigned, but saying those words aloud jolts it back out.

"It's not a submarine. *Salacia* is a submersible. The largest and finest ever built. She has excavation and weapons capability. She can capture, house, and transport creatures that heretofore have only been suited to survival at the basest seabed and safely bring them to our world. In sum, *Salacia* is designed, to the minutest detail, to irrevocably alter the course of human history."

"Thanks, but I just realized I'm a severe landlubber."

"So there *are* limits to your desire to see Angelica?"

"Just critical thinking."

"Love to hear it, but *briefly*."

"This is your third attempt. I think you needed Angelica to help you overcome an obstacle, likely due to her work on artificial intelligence and human consciousness. She was either never willing to share or grew unwilling, at which point you kidnapped her, forcibly extracted what you needed, then eventually killed her. My work on this was somehow annoying you, I don't flatter myself that it was much more than that, so you made one of her last acts consist of helping you stage a suicide so Carlotta would give up the ghost. When you say I will see Angelica if I get in that sub, I believe you. Knowing you, you preserved her in some glass case that lies in the trench as some totem of mankind's evolution from its oceanic source or something. Me seeing her will consist of seeing her lifeless body just before being deposited there myself."

"Not bad. You took your liberties as usual, but there is a definite mental fertility there, no question."

"Enough that I won't be getting inside any sub."

"You're adorable, Riv, you know that? This whole time you think I've been trying to convince you to get inside the *Salacia*? Understand that this vessel is about to have its fuse lit so it can be forcefully launched into the corpse of all it means to be human. You will be accompanying us on this trek. What modicum of agency you have here can be stated simply. You can travel inside the *Salacia 3* with the rest of us. Or you can come lashed to the outside of it like Ahab on his whale."

Inside the submersible, it's somehow true that you can see perfectly well what lies outside, as if its walls were made of glass. We're near the surface but shooting forward briskly. We must be descending as well, because it's getting darker. The ocean is where light goes to die, its advance can only penetrate so far.

If the *Genesis* poet is to be believed, everything was once dark formless void. Until God bathed it in light.

Now the *Salacia 3* is engineering a reversal of that foundational process. What light remains weakens and weakens as I struggle to imagine the nothing that came before anything.

This goes on and on, and when I remember to go back to tracking the dying of the light, there's none left to measure.

On monsters, how critical to the concept is the element of make-believe? Mondragon is asking rhetorically but it's also clear he wants to engage me on this. Only I've decided I'm all talked out.

A lifetime of talking has only landed me here. In a sinking metal tube with constricting walls and no sane destination. And like a prehistoric or maybe posthistoric harvester of the sea, this relentless sub and its demented crew are collecting the vilest creatures conceivable and displaying them in special tanks right near where I sit in a frozen trance.

"You see," he says. "People don't draw a distinction between fictional monsters and factual ones. Instead, skittish humans make it a necessary part of the concept of a monster that it be ultimately attributable to human imagination. You appreciate, I assume, the sleight of hand involved. Feel free to imagine your worst, we're told, because you can always retreat to the safety of reality. *Salacia 3* is going to puncture all that. I mean would you do me the favor of looking upon these literally goddamned creatures arrayed before you?"

It proves difficult to do that. This one thing I'm looking at is a squid-like shark I guess, but with a brutal unending spear for a snout. It's constantly unlocking its jaw in the most unnatural way possible to create an opening basically the size of its body. This means it can swallow the world if necessary. And if you're curious about its internal machinations, just look for yourself because its skin is repulsively translucent.

Another petrifying creation is like some giant sea spider, aortic red with an impossibly wide and flat fish mouth that can't accommodate its sheer plenitude of fangs, so numerous they needily protrude out in anticipation.

Or the crustacean-looking aberration with rows of claws and grasping serrated antennae.

These are some of the more attractive creatures Mondragon's managed to acquire so far.

The struggle to breathe, I swear the sub is contracting in on itself. That sensation when you realize the impossibility of unseeing something you've just seen. I can't control the shaking of my body, I'm just left to try and guess how visible it is to onlookers.

"Okay, what about them?"

"Spot the commonality for me, Riv. What do these accursed life-forms share?"

"Scary choppers?"

"Christ, I gave you the quintessential hint. They are all *life*-forms, as I said, so what they share is life. And above all it is that substance, life, that makes them so terrifying."

"I can think of other elements that contribute more."

"No. Think of Victor Frankenstein. Our modern Prometheus was determined, whatever the cost, to ignite life back into death. He saw only the potential majesty in that. Until one precise moment. Correct, the moment he actually achieved it.

"Shelley tells us that Frankenstein instantly viewed his success as a catastrophe. The mere sight of his creation, what she calls the *aspect* of the being, causes him to flee in horrified disgust. We know there was nothing more to it than that because the creature at that point lacks the power of speech nor has it engaged in any activity.

"Now, if Frankenstein is reacting solely to the monstrous appearance of his creation, what conclusions can we draw from that telling fact? You might be tempted to say that the creature's appearance was just that hideous. But that ignores some primary truths. First, Frankenstein had been staring at precisely that physical appearance for at least months if not years. Remember that he had painstakingly constructed the body himself. More than that, we are told that the body's features had been selected for their beauty.

"So what happened? Put simply, life. Life in all its multidimensional terror happened. Frankenstein himself tells us that the instant he successfully injected life into those recombinant parts, they became a living wretch so hideous even Dante could not have conceived of it.

"Now cast your eyes back on the aspects of those creatures you have been doing your able best to avoid. Recognize the phenomenon?"

I can't *not* look at these creatures when triggered that way. And damn it all to hell if this whoreson bastard doesn't have a point. A still life of these creatures would be disturbing enough, but this . . . the motion. So, yes, the fact that they're alive. That this isn't just a warped attempt to group as many disparate necrotic elements together as possible. This is reality, with all that follows from that.

"See it now, Riv? I think you do. So let's keep drawing conclusions. The fact that life is the ingredient that transports us from quiet nature to the realm of terror is a vital clue to what life is at the level of essence. Judge a creator by its creation. And while you are doing that, contemplate what must be the fundamental nature of that creator's most powerful tool."

He is walking toward me. His aspect, it seems to grow in size and reach as he approaches. He gestures at the tank nearest me.

"Take a moment to suffer once more the vexed countenance of this particular evil monster. Look closely. What message are we being sent?"

Just then, marine biologist–looking staff bring in their latest acquisitions. One is like a large pink vat, a perfectly see-through vessel for displaying intestinal and other decay. Then a seven-foot beast of a shark eel or eel shark with disconcerting frills where gills should be and dead scrotal eye sockets.

"Here now is something," according to Mondragon. "The lizard shark. Our first living fossil. Do you appreciate the import of that?

"Yes, import all over the place."

"Mentally travel with me back in time as we breathe in the presence of this brute who has remained virtually unchanged for eighty million years. A perpetual killing machine who hourly proves his divine perpetuity."

"If you say so."

Another brave-new-world mariner walks in timidly.

"Say hello to Kingsley, Riv. What say you, sir?"

"Less than an hour to our nadir, Your Excellency."

"Is that the update you think I want from you?"

"No sign of it yet."

"And I need you to tell me that? I am perfectly capable of looking in these tanks and concluding that there is no sign of the Lernaean Hydra. And yet you must be aware, aware on practically a cellular level, how entwined your immediate viability is with this being. As I said, we either return with this denizen of the deep in tow or we leave you behind to pursue it on your own."

Mondragon waves his hand and the room clears, leaving just us two.

"Hydra? Like from Greek mythology?" I say.

"You a fan as well?"

"They don't exist. You've given that poor man an impossible task then made death the penalty for failure. I need to lodge a moral objection here."

"An unfounded one. Of course hydras exist. If they didn't, you wouldn't know what I was talking about, with the multiple heads and their ability to regenerate."

"Fine, they exist. But merely as concepts."

"And pray tell where concepts come from?"

"This one comes from us, we like to make shit up."

"Don't give our powers of invention too much credit. Here's what I mean. Think of long-ago depictions of concepts like space aliens. Notice any similarities between those and our rogues' gallery here? I suppose one could attribute it to uncanny coincidence. But attribution properly belongs to a form of memory. A kind of institutional memory, but with the institution being our species. And this is no less true of your ancient Greeks when they sat down to invent, or so they thought, their monsters."

"Oh, God. Is this sub getting smaller, or just for me?"

"We came from the ocean, all of us. We may be the highest iteration of life, but it was the ocean that, three and a half billion years ago, invented life itself that we might then polish it remorselessly. So today we gaze out at the sea, even invade its heretofore impregnable depths, but more than that we *remember* the sea. We remember it the way infants remember their amniotic sacs."

"They certainly do not."

"And it is remembrance, not imagination, that engenders your Lernaean Hydra and the like."

Some more specimens are brought in and they're somehow worse.

We keep descending. And our descent brings decreasing space and breathable air.

It feels like the sub itself is dying and, worse, is resigned to that fact.

"So what then? All this just to create the world's most dreadful aquarium?"

"Funny, but no. All *this*, as you call it, to rid the world of any remaining consolatory artifice. We are monsters because we descend from monsters and we descend from monsters because we are monsters. Turns out Seneca, the Roman philosopher, was right. I will breed and propagate monsters until they constitute a preponderance. I will do this because, as he intuited, monsters are *a visual and horrific revelation of the truth*. Do you refuse to embrace the truth, Riv, is that it?"

"I don't think so. Here's some truth as I see it. These creatures here are hideous to look at, sure. But they're not monsters. And I don't just say that as if in their defense either. I'm saying they are incapable of being monsters.

"Physical appearance is evidence of nothing. Your captives look the way they do because that's what it takes to thrive down here at these lunatic depths. To make a genuine monster you need moral judgments and decisions.

"Frankenstein's monster was no monster at birth, you said so yourself. Was Victor made it so. Spray ammonia on plants instead of water and eventually they'll become monstrous. Frankenstein delivered only isolation and cruelty to his creation, and in response it became a murderer, a monster.

"But that's a low-level monster, right? Think of our historic monsters. I don't know, pick one at random, Exeter Mondragon, say. Those monsters make themselves. And the one thing you don't do when faced with one of these is explain them to themselves; you just end up flattering them if you do that. Because you will inevitably rely on classic human obligations like truth-telling. Truth in all three timelines, about the past, the present, but also about the future, like when we make a promise or enter into an agreement.

"The mistake is that these obligations don't apply to them. As I said, these considerations are *human*. But your audience is inhuman. And by that I mean they are less than human, inferior."

"Did you enjoy that little rant? It sure looked like you did. Okay, let us thrice and for all remove this element. Carnicero!

Bring us the promised proof that our friend's cousins were released, yes? Then, Riv, we can turn to this grand encounter, maybe even contretemps, you believe you are going to have with Angelica."

Hearing that Carnicero name again is bad enough. Worse is the sensation that comes over me now. That the world outside this sub is just dated invention.

"Ah, here we are."

Enter Carnicero and he looks worse. I would not have thought that possible, but in addition to all his preexisting physical improprieties, he is now further undone by an odd yellow sheen to him. At Mondragon's directive that he affix me with extreme prejudice to where I sit, he cuffs my hands behind my back and to a pipe. He leaves.

"Now, Riv. You accuse me of failing to keep a promise. Worse, you hint that I do not even recognize the concept. Yet here is the promised proof that I *released* your cousins."

He gestures at a screen. At this gesture my heart loses the time badly.

"But first allow me a brief word on an unexpected feature of human biology."

I am crying. Not bawling or anything. But it's not like an individual tear can register the difference anyway. Must be my heart.

"If asked to name the most immediate form of human death, I suspect a great many would name decapitation."

The cuffs I wear must have a razor quality to them because my attempt to break free and rush forward is met only by the sensation of warm blood pouring down my hands. I hope it's from the most essential veins and that they empty with the force of a waterfall taking the curse of life with them.

"They would be wrong, these people. Because there is ample support for the notion that both head and body continue to function for a bit even after they have parted company for good. I myself have witnessed this phenomenon rather often, truth be told.

And I can tell you that it is not rare to watch an unmistakable expression of pain and horror form on a just then disembodied face. Think of that as we watch this together."

My body is exactly like that now, empty of everything but reflex.

"Oh, you don't want to see it? How else will you confirm that I am speaking the truth?"

«—»

"I see. You believe me. But you think I lied when I said I released your cousins. What was it again? Fernando? Mauricio? Two fewer del Rios is what I know."

«—»

"But what could be truer than my claim that I released them? Look at you right now, for example. Do you deny that your existence at this moment is like a burden?"

«—»

"Yoked around your neck. Our shared albatross. Are you praying for release?"

«—»

"Your cousins sure prayed for it at the end. Prayed to me, their god. But unlike your God, who responds to prayers with uninterested abstention, I answered in the affirmative. Want to know why?"

«—»

"Just as well. There is no why. Only power and the powerless."

Black is at the same time the absence of color and the sum of all colors.

Same room. Same everything. Same genocidal maniac. Same impotence. Same diminishing air. Same indelible stains on the universe traceable to their broken author. Same author. Same me and my same actions. Same sameness.

"Shame. Did you know, Riv, that it's possible to die of a broken heart? Not a malfunctioning heart, of course you of all people know what that is. I mean the state we refer to when we say he or she has a broken heart. It's a medically recognized condition and we all know of someone who vaguely fits the description. What I long to see is for someone to die from it with the immediacy of a gunshot to the head or a slit throat. I bring it up because until just this second I was hopeful that I was maybe seeing it in you. Alas, it appears I will have to be more proactive."

«—»

"But first, I have one last promise to fulfill. See? I am a human of my word, as you claim to greatly prize. I am going to step aside and give you your long-awaited audience with Angelica. You should make it fitting of your last such intercourse. Then I will be the last face you ever see. I will call your time of death. I will be further tasked with identifying a cause of death. And I will be writing down that you died of insufficient will. Because in the final analysis your undoing will be that my will greatly eclipsed your will. Wouldn't you say?"

"No. I would not. I would say instead that you should free me from these cuffs. Then we can see who outwills who."

The sound just then!

The sub is failing.

I know because I just got drenched with a wave of seawater to the chest, I can taste the salt.

Mondragon takes two steps toward me then pitches forward onto his face without saying a word.

Where Mondragon once stood now stands a fully nude woman posed in replacement.

Above her head, like a halo, I notice a neon ⌒•⌐ for the first time as it starts to flicker.

She seems sculpted. Not tall or big or small or thin or really even capable of that kind of categorization. It's more like she would be the future reference point for concepts like those.

Her hair is like a bed of uncolored snakes. In her left hand, a dagger. In her right, a round device that she holds up from cables as if raising a trophy scalp.

Angelica Alfa-Ochoa.

She is walking toward me.

It's not seawater, it's blood. Mondragon's blood and so much more are copiously on me.

The sub is not failing. Mondragon is at my feet on the floor but staring intensely up at me. His eyes are open and fixed but there's nothing behind them now. It feels like one of the most lurid sights the universe will ever produce.

As I stare back at his emptying face, Angelica's bare foot lands on it then pivots forward so she can step over him and to me. Now she is bringing the dagger to my face. Just when I most steel myself to be stabbed she replaces the blade with her index finger then uses it to wipe something off my lips.

"You had some Mondragon on you."

«—»

She walks away.

"You're welcome," she says.

I am done. I'm all out of reactions, and not just external ones.

—Me imagino que tendrás un mar de preguntas —she says.

Questions. To have them I would need coherence.

"Not a one?"

"Can you put some clothes on?"

"Sure, I think I saw some fig leaves around here." She drops a thin white dress onto herself. "Was that your sole question, then?"

"So relieved to see you this way."

"What way? Clothed?"

"Safe?"

She bats her eyelashes as her lips start to pucker. "You want me to say you saved me, Riv?"

"Seems you saved yourself."

"And you as well, no? Your damsel in shining armor."

"But why don't you seem worried?"

"What, me worry?"

"Yes."

"What about?"

"That Mondragon's crew is about to rush in here, see their leader's condition, and avenge his death at your complete expense."

"Hmm. Mondragon's crew, you say. What's that?"

"His crew. This sub's crew, if you prefer. The people who work for Mondragon and are currently taking us deeper into the ocean than anyone's ever been. I assume they'll be investigating that painful noise any second."

"Oh, I see your point. Yeah, they don't exist anymore."

"What does that mean, they don't exist? There's like twenty of them, I watched them get on."

"Come on, Riv. They existed when you watched them get on the sub. They don't exist now when you ask me if I'm worried about them."

"How? You?"

"So *two* more questions, now you're full of them. Okay, the how. The unaided human body requires that the air it breathes consist of about twenty percent oxygen. Have you ever wondered how it's possible to productively breathe in a sub that's close to seven miles deep into the ocean?"

"No."

"You all kill me. You just take it on faith. What happens is the limitless seawater that surrounds us is put through a process called electrolysis that produces oxygen. As you can imagine, something like the oxygen saturation levels of the various compartments of this craft is closely monitored and controlled. Anything that is controlled can be manipulated."

"You asphyxiated everyone."

"You say that like I did something shameful. These were mur-derers."

"All of them? Some seemed like science geeks all excited at the prospect of slaking their thirst for knowledge."

"Oh, really? What was Mondragon slaking with your cous-ins? Or have you forgotten that already?"

"It's a fake. Confirm that, please. Please just confirm that for me. Then kill me, I don't care."

"You believe it's a fake?"

"He said Fercho prayed to him, bullshit. If he says Mauro did, maybe. But I wouldn't pray to that fuck and Fercho's twice the man I am and a thousand times the believer."

"Torture is torture."

"No, the tortured is all. On second thought, no del Rio would pray to that garbage."

"I don't know the answer to your question, sorry. I do know that the face you made just now when you concluded that I killed everyone was unjustified. Besides, I didn't asphyxiate *everyone*. We're having this conversation, aren't we?"

"You couldn't do this room. And that's where Mondragon and I have been the whole time."

"You're looking at us like enemies, Riv, also unjustified. What can I do to disabuse you of that notion?"

"You have the key to these bracelets?"

"I do not. But I suspect . . . let me see."

She's approaching me again. The way she walks. I need to get on point here. I've changed my mind yet again and now wish to survive this. She's dropped the dagger but still has the device.

She's at the cuffs now and that device makes no more sense for its proximity. She does something wavy with the cuffs and they release me.

"Thought so," she says. "Trick cuffs. Say what you want about him, he did have a flair for the grand gesture. Things I couldn't even envision imagining, if I'm being honest."

"Namely?"

"Imprisoned by an assumption. Like we all are, I'm sure he would've said."

"So if we're not enemies would you mind terribly putting down that device?"

"This? What's it to you?"

"You mean besides the fact that I watched you use it to explode a prodigious man from his inside?"

"So sensitive. But to answer your question, no, I won't be putting it down. Because although I have truthfully told you that we are not enemies, I cannot be sure that you believe me. Or, worse, maybe you believe that is how I feel but you pointedly disagree."

"And?"

"And despite appearances, I am not particularly capable in a physical contest. So I need this to even the odds, you might say."

"What is it, can you at least tell me that?"

"I don't even think it has a name yet, it's so new. But I can tell you what it does. The human body has a very pronounced electrical component. Now, by altering the voltage patterns of a person's cells—"

"Never mind, I get the picture. Here's a more urgent question. We share a strong interest in this submarine—"

"Submersible."

"—in this *craft*, resurfacing into the larger world, preferably in New York Harbor, as I will never again be leaving that city as long as I live. How is that going to happen without a crew?"

"Right."

"We do share that interest, don't we?"

She is sitting at a keyboard typing, and I try my best but can't help but look over at Mondragon. But for Angelica's partial footprint, his face isn't all that changed if I think about it. Even without animation it is a frightening visage.

I just thought there would have been more to his death is all. Not sure what I expected specifically. Maybe a kind of death rattle by the universe that created him. Instead just the sound of Angelica striking keys and an ambient declaration by all there is that this death changes nothing. Still, his stare is landing heavily on my eyes at the moment. I take off my shirt and place it over his face.

"Angelica?"

"Yes."

"On the crucial question of how we get home now that I have valiantly rescued you."

"Right, I forgot. You're worried about our lack of a crew as if we are on the *Andrea Doria* or something. But this crew you were so fond of had about as much to do with the movements of the *Salacia 3* as the croissant Mondragon had for breakfast. Feel me, as the kids say?"

"Yeah, our lives are in the hands of some corny autopilot, think I preferred the demon. So it sets the record for deepest depth or whatever then returns whence it came?"

"I guess."

"We're guessing now? What are you typing in there?"

"Just a slight course correction, you'll agree circumstances have changed."

"But you share my priority, returning safely as soon as possible?"

"It's complicated."

"It's actually not. If you have the ability to alter our course, and it's very much seeming you do, then please do so as quickly as possible to abandon all this Mariana Trench nonsense and get us back to where humans belong, out of this drink and onto lovely dry land."

"It's not that easy. Mondragon was not a man who tolerated a plan B. If this submersible doesn't attain a minimum depth, I'll let you guess what that is, it will not reverse course for the surface."

"You're saying you can't overrule the autopilot?"

"Please stop calling it that. The *Salacia 3* is being operated by the most advanced computational force ever birthed."

"Great. We should be tiptop, then. So long as it doesn't need to recognize a traffic light, or motorcycle, or script."

In my limited remaining time I am apparently doomed to never again encounter a normal human being.

"All set," she says rising from the keyboard.

"Set for what, though?"

"Success, set for success."

"I was hoping for greater specificity. You said you made a slight course correction. Care to share in precisely what manner our course was corrected?"

"You're too close a listener, I think. For your purposes what matters is that our ultimate destination remains unaltered. Lovely dry land, I believe you called it."

"Now who's listening too closely?"

"I don't understand."

"Sorry, I'm just very nosy, occupational hazard."

"I very much like questions, Riv, but the bigger kind. This is minutiae."

"Minutiae? In my view, where this death tube is headed couldn't possibly signify more."

"But I have the opposing view. You concede there are only two views left on this submersible. And you have made obvious your understanding that mine belongs to the only person left who has any chance of safely navigating us home. I guess I just don't think that the fact that a vessel's itinerary changes slightly when a new captain takes over is worthy of much discussion. Especially when there's so much pressing to be attended to."

"Like? You said yourself there's no stopping this thing from sinking to a record low. So what all is it requires your careful maritime ministrations?"

"The record depth is inalterable, the ultimate destination remains the one you most crave. But in between those two events there is room for some improvisation."

"Let's say there's room for it, fine, where's the need for it?"

"I don't understand."

"What's behind the course correction?"

"That kind of question. I don't. Ask a different type."

"Okay, exactly what does the course correction consist of? What will we be doing, or where will we be going, that wasn't part of the original plan as laid out by Mondragon?"

"Mondragon?"

"Yeah, remember him? Now that he's no longer around to direct the sub, what has changed?"

"Direct the sub? You kidding? Human input into operation of the *Salacia 3* was minimal when Mondragon was alive, it is nonexistent now."

"Fine, some AI, then."

"Artificial intelligence, really? Are you a child? An SHC is firmly in control of this vessel."

"Why is that?"

"Why? I don't . . ."

"Just why is all."

"Again, you and I are not enemies in this."

"I agree. And a great way to demonstrate that is by answering my original question. What, if anything, has changed in terms of this sub's mission?"

"I cannot disclose that at this time. Maybe later, before the end." She grabs tighter hold of the nameless device.

"Fair enough. I'm not trying to be confusing. You have a point, all I should really care about is this thing's seaworthiness."

"What are you asking?"

"Nothing really. I guess I'm just hoping you'll rush in with verbal reassurance that the *Salacia 3* remains a potent machine fully capable of executing its primary mission."

"What's that as you see it?"

"Returning two blameless souls to the loving embrace of sufficiently oxygenated nature."

She kind of laughs, I think, not sure.

"The *Salacia 3* remains a potent machine," she says.

"It won't fail?"

"Humans fail, an SHC does not."

"A what?"

She leaves.

Maybe she left the device behind. She did not. The dagger I do find nearby and quickly pocket.

On the screen will be answers.

No, a screensaver that refuses to stop saving the screen.

I want to learn but nothing wants to be learned. The other monitors are all black and it's not like there's an owner's manual around.

I know why I'm so unsettled. Because every little thing is going to be all right, I tell myself. And the novelty of that can throw a person off.

Angelica did what she did because it was either that or suffer a grim death. And she's just really good at hiding her distaste for those necessary actions. Her reticence to share the new plan is understandable given all the poor innocent babe has been through. Innocent like all of us. This whole thing is just a big misunderstanding.

I dreamt I was awake and awoke into a dream.

To learn, first remember.

An unwilling Angelica across from you is useless as a resource. But I cannot forget that I had established a set of suggestive facts about her long before this.

* * *

Now I walk among the dead. The air seems fine, but I did not think Angelica had undone so many. I think how everyone lying there had a history every bit as complex as mine, at least from their perspective.

These bodies are empty vessels now, no one can doubt it, but emptied of what? And what of their acts and omissions? From when they had the power to act and omit. Are those empty now too?

Bottom line is she doesn't seem concerned about her safety at all. She trusts this third *Salacia* and she knows a hell of a lot more about it than I do.

Also she could have exploded me on the cellular level or whatever, like she did Mondragon, when I sat there defenseless thinking I was cuffed. She didn't. She didn't because she means me no harm. And even if she did, even with that tool, she would need the element of surprise, and I doubt anything will ever genuinely surprise me again.

The next room I walk into has no other bodies, human or otherwise, only mine. Again the walls are like windows and the light we carry is illuming sights never intended for human eyes.

If perfectly null silence were visible, it would look like this.

But then I briefly see the loud remains of everyone ever died at sea.

I look away.

There's a gauge. We are currently resisting fifteen thousand pounds of pressure per square inch. Every pound of that is assaulting every inch of me as I locate other monitors that are actually monitoring and dutifully reporting their findings.

I stare and memorize, even those terms and figures that make not a stitch of sense in the moment.

"Can you appreciate, Riv, the magnitude of what we are seeing? Or are you still blinded by mistrust?"

"Trust is famously earned, how are the oxygen saturation levels in here?"

"All such levels have been restored to their proper percentages, see for yourself."

"I see some numbers and words that declare as much, but presumably this very same monitor was making similar declarations throughout to many who now lie lifeless."

"I see what you mean, but you can trust this reporting. Same way you can trust me. Ask me anything."

"You seem most comfortable when I'm asking you questions, why is that?"

"I am very comfortable answering questions."

"But why?"

"Because I know everything."

"Untrue."

"Try me."

"Here's a question. What haven't you had any questions for me?"

"Seems obvious. You want to know things and I can help. There's nothing I need to know from you."

"Nothing? No curiosity centered around, I don't know, Carlotta Ochoa, maybe?"

"You think you can provide me facts about my mother that I don't already possess?"

"I do. For example, if asked, I can tell you the state she was in when she first related the story of your disappearance to me."

"My mother is many things, some good, some bad, but one thing she is *not* is unpredictable. If I tried hard enough I could probably repeat some of her exact words to you."

"I could also tell you the level of credence she attached to that little fake letter you created."

"Beyond what I can deduce from the fact that a funeral was subsequently held in my honor? And don't you mean the letter Mondragon created?"

"I do not. Don't you want to know what your mother's face looked like as she had to ghoulishly choose between believing that her daughter had been murdered in the most violative way possible or that she had taken her own life, with all that act entails for those left behind? Don't you especially want to know this given that the brutal choice you forced on her was a choice between two lies?"

"This is a remarkable turn. A letter *I* faked? A choice between lies that *I* forced on her? How quickly the dead are forgotten these days. I vanquished Mondragon. I ended that atrocity machine, not you. Are you saying this means that machine's past misdeeds become mine as a result?"

"I'm saying if you're the new boss, you're at least redolent of the old one."

"A man creates the most powerful and pervasive criminal network the world will ever see. A young female scholar is ensnared in his world against her will and must then do whatever's necessary to survive. If you want to share the mental gymnastics you underwent to arrive at the kidnapped girl being to blame, I will listen closely."

"Everything you're saying should be hitting me with the unique force of truth."

"Correct."

"But it somehow isn't."

"Is that right? So what is the truth as you see it?"

"Well, I'm not quite ready to label it truth just yet, more like instinct or intuition, but educated."

"And?"

"And I don't think you're a kidnapped girl, neither of those things. I think you're brilliant, but in a really uninteresting way. Through that brilliance, however, you've acquired some very specialized expertise. It relates to artificial intelligence or this other nonsense and it runs very deep. I read your early proposal on the general subject and understood what I could, you're no skilled popularizer.

"But it's not just deep expertise either; you're emotionally invested. I saw the offense you took when I disparaged your baby, it went beyond the passion of the connoisseur to that of the zealot."

"None of that means I wasn't kidnapped."

"True. But other considerations mean that. Your father once worked for Mondragon. I figured that out by applying the transitive property to a slew of shell companies culminating in the sale of his company and its intellectual property to a corporate entity bizarrely named Rilke of Gold. This name, I later gather, an anagrammatic reminder to its secret owner that he is the Killer of God. And if you think the name is odd, you should see the logo of a gold-colored Rainer Maria staring at a giant black arc over a black dot. The very arc and dot symbol, it turns out, that decorates this vessel inside and out and just seems to be everywhere once you know to look for it.

"I make no extensive claims about your father beyond that. Far as I can tell, he sold out and worked for Mondragon for the same reason everybody works for someone, money. In the case of your father, a great deal of it. Much of that work, initiated long ago, took the form of a super vague and secretive AA Project. Code named, I now realize, after you, Angelica Alfa."

"How flattering."

"Mondragon needed your expertise for this God-forsaken descent we're currently enduring. Your father is the height of unavailable, but you continued and probably exceeded his work. So he paid you to contribute and come along. No violence, no kidnapping, just the primary and maybe eternal lubricant of all human malice."

"I see, so add avaricious to brilliant and uninteresting on my list of qualities."

"No. I said he paid you, I didn't say that was your true motivation."

"So what's your educated intuition about *that*?"

"Your motivation? I know this, it ran counter to Mondragon's. I saw firsthand the proof of that, some of it is still on me."

"You think that is how I handle differences of opinion?"

"I think you thought there was room to accommodate your goals within Mondragon's plan. When you realized that wasn't feasible, and maybe you also blame Mondragon for your father's untimely death, you were driven to action. I bet that *minor* course correction you made just now was anything but. It's as major as a life's work gets, even one like yours that's characterized mainly by brevity. In your defense, you also probably correctly suspected that once your utility to Mondragon disappeared so soon would you."

"Thank you, but I wasn't really looking for a defense."

"Point is, whatever grand claim it is you're looking to make on behalf of AI or SHC or anything else, no one cares. What's your next paper going to say about your fieldwork? Hey, MIT guys, I like totally stowed away on the privately built sub of some criminal maniac with global reach and here are my findings?"

"Papers? MIT? You think I care about any of that?"

"I'm guessing you did when you wrote them. Thing is, it's not *real*, any of it. Here's something real. Turn this sub around. Let's figure out how we deal with reentry given the current contents of this sub and—"

"What does that mean?"

"Have you given no thought to what happens when we return as sole survivors? This network you just took a huge bite out of is known for disproportionately violent repercussions, not so much for the old forgive and forget."

"I've given thought, as you say, to everything. But the more relevance is present, the more I give. Thought you wanted me to focus on the real? Curious as to what you see as real, maybe you'll convince me."

"One real thing, for sure, would be the state of your devoted mother if you were to suddenly appear before her in miraculous flesh."

Her reaction to this is no reaction at all, with zero evidence that one is being suppressed. It's just not a thing to her.

"Aren't you going to correct any of my work, Angelica? Surely even I didn't achieve perfection on my first attempt."

"Well done, your attempt, but it's complicated. And the complexity inures to my benefit, justifying everything I've done."

"Said everyone ever."

"The better practice, you'll agree, would be to withhold judgment until you've heard the truth, the whole truth, and nothing but the truth."

"I'm listening."

"First I'd like to show you something. Follow me, please."

"I don't feel well."

"Certainly you feel well enough to follow me a short distance."

"Tell me again about the oxygen levels."

"They are no longer being tampered with."

"I had my heart set on proof."

"See for yourself . . . again."

I walk over.

"Yes, I see for myself. But show me how you did it. And how I can be sure you stopped doing it and, most importantly, are not currently doing it."

She does and I say I see.

"I see," I say.

She walks into the adjacent compartment and I follow.

The sight out the window in there. Even after everything I've seen. A universe is only as good as its rules. If anything is possible in the physical world, you can never hope to impose order on the rest.

Because we are underwater, that's well established, but I am somehow staring at a genuine waterfall. Its water cascades down with terrific force as if the motion were perpetual and all of it was the elemental engine powering the perfect sum of the universe's activity.

"Can you believe it?" she says.

"Just your basic underwater waterfall, I guess."

"No, not that. Look out there, in the far distance."

"Hell's that? Smoke?"

"That's where you're from. And it'll take some time yet but that's where we're going."

"Smoke and waterfalls and monsters, oh my. Isn't hallucinating a symptom of oxygen deprivation?"

"It is."

"Then you'll excuse my paranoia, but I'm going to check that monitor one more time to be safe."

When I return I can tell I no longer exist to her. She is staring straight ahead from the nose of the sub with her arms outstretched as if initiating an embrace. Music is playing.

"I feel now what the great Magellan must have felt half a millennium ago as his expedition returned whence it originally set sail three years earlier. A triumphant return having broken free of all prior nautical restraints to arrogantly circumnavigate the globe."

Takes me a second to realize she's not talking to me. I shrink my presence even further, as if it would be wrong to spy on the heartless entity marching us into oblivion.

"As humankind plunges into depths and recesses once thought impregnable, this human will claim the dominance over the physical world that is her birthright."

This has the ineffable quality of prepared text, which only ups the discomfort. She sees me and puts her hands down.

"You're back. Presumably armed with greater or restored belief in my good faith?"

"I'm back."

"Tell me what you think of this music."

The music is terrible.

"It's nice," I say.

"Thank you, it's mine. I figured you would be unduly impressed, music being so overrated by you all. Math is the only way to directly address the universe."

"You've accomplished a lot at a young age. This feel like a culmination?"

"You have no idea."

"Give me one . . . an idea."

"I can't."

"Don't sweat it, I was being sarcastic. The fact that someone goes somewhere has never impressed me all that much, never struck me as an accomplishment at all."

"I'm not trying to impress you."

"I understand that. And I concede I'm at a huge informational disadvantage when I say that, to me, this is looking more and more like tourism for the extremely rich than any kind of achievement."

"You're very sure of yourself. But consider that you may be like a snail on a garden hose concluding that the universe is green and tube-shaped."

"And yet I'm one of only two viewpoints left, as you noted. That gives my view the power of equality. And I say fancy tourism."

She sits.

No sign of the conqueror of worlds from a minute ago.

"What you sound like right now. Imagine if the first time one of our ancestors rose to walk on two legs someone like you was sitting nearby saying *big deal, I don't mind scraping my knuckles.*"

"You think that a valid comparison?"

"I do. Let me ask you. Where do you think this ends?"

"I can tell you how it *should* end. The proper ending starts with you going back into that room and instructing this thing to make one of the all-time great U-turns in the history of human travel. I have an intensely bad feeling about our current destination. Call me old-fashioned, but I don't trust underwater smoke and waterfalls."

"I'm not talking about this particular journey by two humans. I mean what is the end of humanity?"

"Aw, fuck off."

"See? I say that and your mind automatically goes to annihilation. But what if instead of annihilation, I am actually referencing evolution?"

"Same answer."

"The human brain is a severely overrated instrument."

"You got a better one?"

"I do. But it's a needy one."

Our progress is slow, a rare thing to be grateful for at the moment.

"You don't want to know what the instrument is, Riv?"

"Correct, I do not."

"SHC, or Supra Hominin Cognition."

"There it is. I'm guessing just a fancier name for AI."

"Bad guess. Supra Hominin Cognition bears approximately the same relationship to AI as space travel does to playing in a sandbox."

"That's fine, I'll stick with the human brain and mind, but thanks for playing."

"Really? I bet that preference is task-dependent. If I told you your life depends on very quickly and accurately calculating the square root of thirty-three to the eleventh decimal, my guess is you would assign that task to an SHC over yourself or any other human."

"And?"

"And that is power, that is supremacy."

"Big deal. If a calculator could think it would never be so good at math."

"But now imagine the most powerful calculator ever built being equally adept at creative thinking. A calculator that knows it's a calculator and can even wonder about what calculators are at their core, their purpose."

"Can't believe you, Angelica. This whole thing's been about worshipping the *Salacia*'s operating system? Let me tell you something. Call it whatever you want, it cannot think. I can think, I'm quite good at it. And I think, hell, I *know*, we are making a beeline right into the heart of natural calamity. I can sense, in every neuron and fiber of my existence, that this is a bad idea. Trust me over that damn machine and let's get the fuck out of here."

"There's a fatal flaw in what you're asking me to do. The *Salacia 3*'s SHC says we head straight for that calamity, as you call it. You want me to overrule that SHC. Problem is, I am the SHC directing the *Salacia 3* thusly."

"Hell does that mean?"

"Where's the ambiguity?"

"You have the SHC? Where?"

"Listen closely. I don't have or control the SHC. I *am* the SHC."

"Okay, is that some kind of attempt at a poetic statement? Like *I am vengeance* or some such shit?"

"No, I am being fully literal."

"You're not an artificial intelligence, Angelica, literal or otherwise."

"I know I'm not."

"You're not a Supra Hominin Cognition either. What do you say you come back to reality before reality assails us both into mincemeat?"

"There you go again with the unwarranted certitude."

"Just believing my eyes. I look at you, I don't see computer. I see flesh and bone and muscle and hair. All things computers and AIs and the like are famous for not having."

"Do you think an AI could ever become self-aware? How about grow a body?"

"No, both of those ideas are nonsense."

"I agree, and yet I say to you truthfully that I am the Supra Hominin Cognate armed with SHC and directing this sub."

"Listen, kid. I'm not down with this little Turing Test bullshit interplay going on between us right now. You think you're an AI or an SHC or an LED? Great, have fun with that. Maybe you are, hell do I know? If you are, I commend you on your brilliant impersonation of a human, top notch. Point is I don't know and I don't care. One thing I am confident in is you have the ability to turn this thing around and I don't. And I am pleading with you to do so immediately. Can you do that for me?"

"I cannot. And I think you have the right to know why that is. I also don't like being thought a liar or lunatic."

"I'm listening. But if the ultimate claim is that you are an AI-type entity that developed sentience, or a machine that is indistinguishable from a human, then save your breath, or digital pulses."

"My father would have liked you. Even if I no longer do. At a minimum he would have agreed with you on your overriding point, although he was a lot more nuanced about it. I know you're familiar with his general parameters. He was a medical doctor. But he was the rare one who wasn't impressed by his abilities. On the contrary. See, for decades he witnessed, at a breath's distance, the depredations of the flesh. And here I'm not just talking about death. There are states worse than death. He watched his mother's personality disappear entirely while her body motored on like a driverless car until her sudden death. He learned his wife could not ever bear children."

"So is that what he agreed with me on? That vulnerable human bodies suck."

"No. I think you agree with him on the majesty of human consciousness and its fundamental irreplicability. We don't know how consciousness arises nor can we fully limn its import and capacities. And how many things can we still say that about at this late stage? My father gave up on those questions rather quickly. He chose instead to just accept that human consciousness and its precursor, life, are simply the universe's optimal miracle, one far beyond the reach of productive human activity.

"Now, understand that he formed these insights against the backdrop of the late twentieth century's explosion in computing. The one that saw twelve-year-olds carrying around computers more powerful than the ones we used to land on the moon.

"More than that, the age featured the dawn of a little thing called the internet. My father took one look at that thing and knew that knowledge, and the power that comes with it, would never be the same. So he knew what computing could grow into, but he also rightly deduced what it could never achieve. That the most powerful force in the universe, human thought, would wield this tool but never the other way around."

Is she angry?

"Unless," she says.

"Unless you let God do most of the work."

"Well put. What my father correctly concluded is that true superbeings would not be computers that could think like humans. They would be humans, with all that entails, with the capacities of computers. Imagine it. The miraculous advances in computing occurring within, literally, the preexisting miracle that is human life and thought. No Turing Test needed because no barrier of meaning to overcome. Just a human being with all the computational power, and all the attendant benefits, of our greatest machines."

"Never happen."

"Silly human. It already happened, a long time ago. I'm just being considerate and catching you up."

"What exactly is it you say happened?"

"The Alpha Angels, or AA Project, happened, that's what. My father conceived and directed the project while Exeter Mondragon unwittingly, very unwittingly, funded it. The project succeeded beyond his wildest imaginings, though death cheated its author from realizing the full extent of that success."

"Succeeded how?"

"You have no doubt heard of the world's first test tube baby, born so long ago now that it's difficult to appreciate the shock at the time. Well, that's cute, but at exactly one second past the first midnight of the year 2000, a woman who science had declared hopelessly infertile gave Cesarean birth to history's first vacuum tube baby. An infant biologically indistinguishable from the infinite multitudes that had come before, save for one critical element. A living, cooing evolutionary leap. The first human with both a mother and a motherboard. Her name?"

"Angelica Alfa."

"Very good. You see now that my father didn't name his AA Project after me. He fittingly named me after the project that culminated in my birth."

"All that so you, his daughter, would be good at calculating?"

"I think you can probably intuit by now that calling a Supra Hominin Cognate good at calculating is as severe as understatement gets."

I look at Angelica now and can't believe I ever thought she was anything but what she now says she is, whatever that is.

"Okay, then," I say. "All that to what end? Can I know that?"

"Why don't we start with a couple means before we get to the end? What about progress? Or evolution? Are you a fan of those concepts at least? Or are those as contemptible to you as that of the artificial intelligence on cosmic steroids that is SHC?

"Because, before you answer that, note that it is inarguable *fact* that I am simply better than even the finest specimen of unenhanced humanity. Take, for example, life expectancy. I am currently predicted, by my operating system, to live until the glorious age of one hundred and forty.

"That's its current estimate, based on my current rate of cellular and organic degeneration and the currently available technology relevant to those factors. I hope I don't need to tell you that as the latter element develops that number will only grow. As for the unforeseen, if anything untoward threatens my peerless health it is immediately detected and combated with extreme prejudice. All the world's medical knowledge is at my disposal, simply because the same is true of all human knowledge period, full stop.

"I know more because I know everything and because I know everything I will live longer and that longer life means I will gain more wisdom and effectiveness. So a more durable and efficient body housing a cerebral instrument orders of magnitude more powerful than any human brain that ever operated heretofore. A First Being indeed. How can anyone view this as anything but the evolution of humankind into better angels?"

"Better at what?"

"Better at everything. What ails you? I mean besides death and ageing, which I just covered. Do you enjoy when one of your peers falls into drunken sleep and drives a school bus into a frozen lake? How about when a collection of similar specimens collaborates on a series of unconscionable errors that cause a nuclear meltdown? Or maybe you like when one diseased purely human brain is able to plunge hundreds of millions into the chaos of warfare. Give me some decades and events like these will be as passé as the horse and buggy."

242 · SERGIO DE LA PAVA

"Yeah, I forgot, every new thing is like the steam engine and it's either going to elevate us into a life of pure leisure or else replace us outright."

"You don't understand, so much incomprehension. This *new thing* makes every previous new thing irrelevant, not just today either but retrospectively. Think of it this way. To what do we attribute a development like the steam engine or the wheel or the internet? Let's call it human ingenuity as shorthand. Well, it's early but as the first-ever product of a kind of in utero microchip-based gene splicing, I am as if human ingenuity itself has just been invented and loosed for the first time to act on the world.

"For you and I to even begin to understand each other, you will have to forget everything you think you remember about the capacities of human intelligence. Because when I get going it will seem as if I am simultaneously recounting the future as if it were past while also, in a sense, speaking it into existence. The quality of thought I am already engaging in means primarily that thought itself will never be the same. Are you beginning to appreciate this?"

"Can I ask you a question?"

"Yes, the point is you can ask me anything that you want me to respond to with knowledge because I know everything, including everything there is to know about knowledge."

"Why are we here?"

"The *Salacia* was originally intended to deconstruct—"

"No, I mean *why* are we here?"

"I thought you were uninterested in hackneyed Turing interplay? Are you really trying to trip me up with a classic ponderous *why* question? Fine, I'll play along. I cannot answer your why question. I know every possible permutation of how, where, and when. But I don't know why. I can't tell you why life instead of no life. Don't know what the grand meaning behind it all is, or even if there is one. An actual deficit, I admit. I cannot solve for all that.

"But guess what? Neither can you! And neither can any of your so-called great thinkers throughout history, by the way. No one or thing can dispositively deal with the *why*s. At least Angelica Alfa and her descendants can master literally everything else. But nice try, Riv."

"What try? There wasn't any more to my question than met the ear. Why are we, Angelica and Riv, here, on a sub, headed to that mess?"

"If it's a mess, then it's a fine mess."

"And I see we've reached the refer-to-yourself-in-the-third-person stage of your evolution."

"That *mess* is anything but. This is the one area of disagreement between me and my father. He threw his hands up in defeat at the prospect of humans creating life and consciousness other than through the one tried-and-true method. True, that concession spurred the remarkable innovations that led directly to you sitting across from a superbeing. But the main reason I am precisely that is my ability to think better and more deeply about questions like this, agree?"

"Disagree."

"And I say he was wrong, although understandably so. Because something once happened, no denying it. Life and consciousness didn't exist and now they do. I know how it happened and I know where it all started."

"That's a hydrothermal alkaline vent, then."

"Very good, you do impress at times."

"That's just a theory about the origins of life, not proven."

"Unenhanced humanity has theories. I have knowledge."

"So what then? We go in there to die at the location of our original birth? Now you sound like Mondragon."

"No one's going to die."

"You can't just mess with the thermal vents as I recall. There's all sorts of sensitive tectonic plates in there and whatnot."

"Okay, I misspoke, many will die. But you and I will be fully protected in here until it's safe to resurface. More importantly, we are going to do things at that site that will redefine the very meaning of existence."

"We?"

"Who else? Unless you're saying you want off this ride. Because that can be arranged."

"What do you mean, many will die?"

"A great many die, every hour of every day, you know this."

"That's not what you meant."

"Do you know that, as we speak, this movement you're so offended by, the *Salacia 3* preparing to deeply penetrate the vent, is purely a matter of nature taking its course? *Salacia* and I have mutually agreed to cease all propulsion for now and instead rely solely on the gravitational pull emanating from the center of the Earth.

"So our work there will be a product of our home calling us back into itself. I am the Eve of this new species, and soon I answer a distress signal more than a quarter century old. I will do so in my capacity as the very first terrestrial angel."

"What signal?"

"The Bloop."

"The what now?"

"In 1997, a bizarre underwater sound was detected by NOAA and never properly explained. My father needed no explanation, he understood its import immediately. I am his answer and it is a resounding yes."

"God help me if I have to listen to any more of this. What did you mean when you said many will die? The truth!"

"Progress, regress, ingress, egress, evolution, elevation, solution, elocution, metonym, metaphor, metamorphosis. These things come at a cost. I don't feel great. I don't want to talk to you anymore."

She sits down.

"What's the cost, Angelica?"

"You wouldn't understand, it takes higher functioning. You're descended from apes, an accident, and seek a meeting of the minds with a descendant of the planar silicon chip, my birthstone, forged in a cauldron of the universe's primary elements."

"The cost, please."

"It's inexplicable."

"I bet. And I also bet, as I learn more about these delusions, that the cost is not a personal one to you."

"What do you care who pays it? Especially since it won't be you. The only question is whether the benefit justifies the cost."

"Keep the benefit to yourself, just interested in a very specific disclosure of this cost you keep referring to."

"I'm sure you've heard of the famous relationship between broken eggs and omelettes. Well, you can't elevate a species to untold heights without leaving behind a chrysalis. So, yes, we will be initiating various processes and collecting certain material and these actions will produce significant effects in the world we temporarily left behind. This is none of your concern so long as you stand by my side."

"Where I'll stand depends on what these effects are."

"That's your problem in a nutshell, isn't it? You will think they are a big deal, the effects, but only because you are a small deal. Earthquakes, some category six hurricanes, these things are insensate occasional events of our physical world. They are not telling factors that should impact our conduct in the slightest."

I simultaneously have no doubt these will be the effects, no possible idea how it can be so, and no curiosity to learn.

"When they occur randomly, maybe, but you're talking about engaging in activity that will directly effect these disasters? Another way of saying that people, innocent people, will die needlessly."

"Innocent people? Where do you keep those? And nothing will happen needlessly. Quite the contrary, they literally need to die and they will."

"That's repulsive."

"And you're just the person to make that determination, right? Tell me, on a related topic, do you think it's repulsive to alter the suicide note of a loved one?"

"What?"

"Just a hypothetical, no need to get so exercised."

"Hell you talking about?"

"I think you know. It's funny. When people think of a category like *all the world's knowledge* they think the components of that are strictly assertible facts about subjects like history or science. But when I said I know everything, I truly meant it.

"So you have your classic easily discernible facts. Like the fact that exactly three days before you landed in Cali, you called 911 from your apartment landline to report an unresponsive forty-eight-year-old woman by the name of Jane Seeds. Or the fact that her death was almost immediately ruled a suicide. These are precisely the kind of facts you would probably expect me to know."

"I don't expect anything of you. And you don't *know* those things. You just have the ability to look them up."

"What do you think knowledge is? A stimulus comes in and it either triggers a whole new set of stimuli, in other words your base of knowledge, or it doesn't. In this case your name arose as someone who was looking for me and I was able to instantly learn these, you'll admit, rather meaningful facts. Note that when I say instantly I mean that I discovered these facts so quickly and seamlessly that the line between learning and knowing was blurred beyond any meaningful distinction. And before you try to downplay all this as just a question of increased speed and efficiency understand that these were effortless and untrammeled searches of databases, the NYPD and the medical examiner's office, that I was in no way authorized to search.

"But I was getting to the worst part for you. Every email you've ever sent. No, any writing you've ever done on a keyboard that wasn't a typewriter, whether you then intentionally sent it anywhere or not. Any web search you ever initiated. Many of the phone calls you've made. Not just the numbers, dates, times, and places involved, the actual substance of the conversations. All this as accessible to me as the meaning of a simple word is to the reader holding a dictionary.

"See now why I say I know everything? Know what I know and you can look into a person's soul. So I repeat my question. Do you think it's repulsive to alter the suicide note of a loved one?"

"Tell you what, let's go back to San Cipriano and we can each answer for our respective deeds there."

"A woman who was always loyal to you."

"I think you mean two people who were always loyal to each other."

"Three years together and that's how you see her off, with a lie. Why won't you look at me? You normally have so much to say."

The sub is barely moving but it feels weird knowing it's being sucked in instead of exercising its will.

"You make me sick, Riv. I don't mean that as a figure of speech either. I actually feel unwell as a result of our talks. Maybe it's being judged by those with no standing to judge. No more of this, engaging with a liar, I have work to do."

"You cannot possibly be serious."

"You drove her to it."

"Am I a child?"

"You deny it?"

"Jane was broken in some ways. Maybe we all are, probably, whatever, but hers happened to align perfectly with the exact vulnerabilities the world is best at assailing. I couldn't fix what was broken, which isn't the same as saying no one could have. I could have been someone else, but who I am kept getting in the way. Did I maybe relent in the end? I guess, but that's the thing about vigilance. If it were common it wouldn't warrant such a powerful name."

She is smiling.

"There are situations can only be understood from the inside, I don't care what words you have access to."

The sub is getting smaller again.

"I didn't want her last act to be steeped in spite. She had good, she *was* good. She just had a lot of pain. And the worst kind, the kind that can't be convincingly attributed to anything external.

"The note was her at her worst. Those times when she would take the pain inside her and just try to expel it onto others. But for every time she did that she bore it like steel a hundred times over.

"Two words into that note and I can tell, this is Jane as inflictor of pain. Her meager family is going to come in from corny Wisconsin, read that, and suffer the special enduring pain of unfair accusations that can never be countered because the dead outrank us all.

"So, yeah, I changed it. Jane was brilliant, maybe her primary affliction, but she never fully trusted herself as a writer. She sometimes relied on me to best put things into words for her or would often ask me to proofread to the point of editing. So I just did it one last time for her."

"Interesting."

"One last time so she could rest without guilt."

"You believe that?"

"It's not a question of belief. I know what I did and why I did it."

"I meant the soul part."

"You better hope you're right that there's no such thing as a soul."

"What makes you think I don't believe in the human soul?"

"Silly me, guess I can't help but make assumptions about someone ready to kill thousands on a whim. Believers in souls tend to want to take better care of theirs than that."

"Listen, this has gone on too much, too much time. We have physical acts to complete."

"*We* don't have anything. Save for an irreconcilable difference."

"If you value self-preservation at all, Riv, you and I share everything."

"How can I make you understand that you cannot intentionally cause many human deaths?"

"The current projection is—"

"No, you want to give me a number but I want you to understand something even more basic than that. I want you to understand that every human death, even the most unsurprising and timely one, radiates out misery and suffering and desolation. That they accumulate until it feels the darkness will ultimately prevail over the light. You don't contribute to that."

"And I want you to understand that I don't care. I don't care about humanity and never really have. This is so much bigger than all that and, frankly, you should be grateful for your extremely privileged view of this development and your role as handpicked documenter, instead of doing whatever this is."

"Yeah, my luck is extraordinary, it just happens to flow in the wrong direction."

"You used that word, not me. Luck is an invention of unenhanced humanity if ever there was one. You all love to shift blame. I love truth, and the more I look at the math, the less I believe in accidents. Example, your presence here."

"Now you're going to explain my presence here? To me?"

"Consider, you wrote a suicide note as Jane Seeds. I had perfect access to that note, as well as to every other thing of note you two had written, to each other and otherwise. I knew the words you used in every text you ever sent her and in the ones she sent you, three years' worth of data. I knew the way you liked to combine those words, your style, if you want to use a misleading word."

"So?"

"So I wanted to disorient you subliminally. I quoted extensively, you two and high-profile others, to compose a pretend somewhat suicide note from Angelica. Angelica doing Riv doing Jane doing famous suicides doing timeworn allusive phrases tailored to their true audience, you. If you want to reliably attract someone, look like them, talk like them, adopt their mannerisms, I'm doing some of it right now. I parroted you back at you and it was enough to persist naggingly and lure you here."

"No, I came here to find out what happened to you because I promised I would. I made that promise to your mother. You know, the woman who devoted her life to you and who you have been torturing mercilessly."

"I know you want to think that."

"No, I *know* that's why I'm here. Just like I know I wouldn't gratify my ego at the expense of innocent human life."

"And yet you'll watch as I do just that."

"No."

"You're going to close your eyes?"

"No, my eyes are wide open and will stay that way. The better to prevent you from doing anything evil."

"Prevent? You see what comes from humoring people too long? I wanted you here because I thought it would be stupendous if someone from the species being discarded was able to document its obsolescence in real time, especially if they had a talent for documenting. But that . . . just a thought really. Don't start thinking you have a greater role in this than you do."

"Don't worry, I won't overestimate my role. Especially because I can't tell you how honored I am that you trust me with such a momentous assignment. The story of how the world's first human computer computed so well she forgot to be human."

"Human you say? Human, like Exeter Mondragon? Like you? If you could only appreciate how silly you sound right now. It's my fault you were born of a lie and into another? That you continually diverted your eyes from the ample precedential proof around you?"

She takes a deep breath.

"Do you know anglerfish, Riv? If I were you I would start to inform myself on that grim topic. There are even some in the next room if you want a visual reference. They operate in a manner that, to your ears, will sound bizarre but is actually on the precipice of becoming the way of the world. And this, even more than their horrific appearance, is the most fitting emblem I can think of for this new world I am about to usher in."

I look closely at her face, its color.

"Not so," I say.

"The Fanfin Sea Devil."

"Keep it to yourself, please. I've had my fill of devils."

"Ever wonder how it ensures propagation of its species?"

"All the time. But I prefer to keep wondering."

"The female devils are very romantic. When a suitable male appears and approaches, and understand that the females they approach outsize them by about a factor of ten, he understands his role perfectly. He bites into the female. But this is supplication, not aggression.

"Because the bite will ultimately lead to a subsumption. See, the bite bonds the male to the female so that the male can fulfill its destiny as a kind of parasite. This is perfect bondage. The male disappears as an independent entity. The female's circulation replaces its own. More than that, its very tissue and skin are replaced by its master. The subservience is complete.

"A female can swim around with eight of these mindless servants fused to its body, all at the ready to be activated if needed. If not, they can remain emptied shells. You're good at subtext. Are you capturing this one?"

"I think so."

"Good. Because you said before that your inventions either liberate or replace you. You omitted what your inventions actually most often do in relation to their inventors: they enslave. How else would you describe a human not yet six months old transfixed by a portable screen that other children built?"

"Making you what? My master?"

"Stop struggling, Riv. A lifetime spent wriggling on the universe's hook as it baits death on your behalf. Think of the imminent liberation awaiting you. Come bite into me. The end of your struggle and the start of transcendence. Come on, you won't feel a thing."

"No thanks. And if there's a parasite in this room it's you, no? You, who needed the unique traits of humanness. And not just the physical body. Imagination, creativity, artistry, a conscience. You can't calculate your way to those things. That's why this music, your music, is so terrible. And that's why I won't be documenting anything on your behalf. Write the document yourself, and don't imitate me either."

"You keep saying these things, I can only assume unintentionally, that only serve to imperil your very existence. You say words indicating that you think you can prevent me from completing my lifelong mission or that you will not be filling the role I envisioned for you. But surely you understand . . . that if I believed either of those things to be true . . . the chances that I would . . ."

She is looking around for something but is not going to find it. The end of every human story is a human not finding what they need in time. But Angelica has had nothing to prepare her for that fact.

"What's wrong, Angelica? Have you misplaced something? Something you need at this very moment?"

"I'm not like you and yours. I don't need things."

"Not even the thing you never bothered to name and that Mondragon reacted so poorly to?"

"What about it?"

"Just that it appeared you were maybe looking for it just now, right around the time you seemed to decide I wasn't going to be all that useful to you after all, maybe even going to be a problem."

"If I conclude you're a problem, you'll know it."

"I'm not trying to be all Delphic. So I'll just say it, I hid the device from you."

"Now why would you go and do a thing like that?"

"Sorry, something about the sight of you with that thing in your hand was needling my trust issues. But I can disclose its location if that helps. I put it the same place I put Mondragon's thumb."

"Congratulations, then. You managed to safeguard your safety. You know who else's safety isn't at issue? Mine. You know full well anything happens to me . . . you would be . . . gone . . . you would be . . . a goner . . . so I can't kill . . . I can't kill you . . . true . . . but neither can you kill me . . . you need me to live if you're to live . . ."

"I know."

"You say I'm going to kill innocent people. Well, you're going to watch me do it. Because the only way to stop me is to kill me, and you can't do that because, like all you worms, all you ultimately care about is self-preservation."

"You okay?"

"All you are about is self-preservation."

"I know."

"At least you admit it."

"I meant that I know you think that. You feel invulnerable because of it. Me? I'm walking talking vulnerability."

"How fun that must be for you."

"But it has its advantages. You begin with the certainty that I cannot kill you and that shuts you off from all sorts of relevant stimuli."

"I see, and had I attended to it all, I would see that you *are* going to kill me?"

"I don't have the stomach for that, no. But I do think we've reached the point where I can safely make you understand the situation you're in and why the only future that serves your interest is one where this fucking tube does a one-eighty and returns to civilization and all its discontents. No one else would die, you and I would part ways forever, and you would live to try and make us obsolete some other day."

"I think you draw way too much significance from the fact that I cannot kill you without use of the device. Not, as you claim, the other way around, with me the one misattributing significance. It's my life that signifies here. Unless you kill me, I am going to complete my mission. But know that if you kill me, *Salacia 3* is just going to keep following its geodesic right straight into the very center of the earth. That would not be a good destination for you. Unenhanced humanity and that location, not an attractive match."

"I hid your murder weapon same place I hid Mondragon's thumb."

"Good for you . . . *what?*"

"Mondragon's thumb. Remember when you separated him from it? I saw it lying there at my feet and picked it up."

"You picked up a disembodied thumb, aren't you full of surprises?"

"See that's the thing about being paranoid. If you always think everyone's out to get you, then on the rare occasion it's true, you're at least prepared."

"You're going to need a lot more than a thumb."

"Well, I'd watched him use its print to gain access to the sub's computer. I had thoughts too. I figured Mondragon and I were alive because we were in the only uncompromised room. But you were also undoubtedly alive and I knew you hadn't been in the room with us. Obviously you'd tampered with *Salacia*'s gauges and displays so that the crew wouldn't know the danger they were in. But that didn't change the fact that the air was actually lethal, but somehow not to you. I know you weren't walking around with any kind of external aid, so I could only conclude you had the internal capacity to adjust things like your nitrogen and oxygen intake to safe levels no matter what poison the *Salacia* spewed into the air.

"When I told you I wanted to check the display in the other room to assure my safety, I used the handy thumb I had to access Mondragon's administrator privileges. I saw how you did it. How you made it so the *Salacia* emitted toxicity while declaring it was producing only suitable air. I then did the opposite. I made it so the air being emitted remained perfectly fine but the attendant numbers spelled disaster for human lungs.

"Where's the harm, right? What do we care if the *Salacia* claims it is slowly choking us to death if it's not actually true? Unless."

"Unless one of our bodies was autonomically reacting to the false information."

"That's an interesting thought, Angelica. Human bodies can certainly be misled into reacting to something that isn't actually present, but for the most part our bodies react to reality. Yet, hypothetically, if there were a quasi-human body with a bizarre unnatural operating system that was receiving and responding to inaccurate data and doing so well outside the scope of con-sciousness, that body could actually do serious harm to itself if, for example, it instituted unnecessary compensatory measures. So if such a body erroneously thought the ambient air contained insufficient nitrogen or excessive oxygen, it might even ironically sicken itself in an attempt to combat a danger that lacked all clarity and presence."

She tries to rise but is too weak.

"You are a stupid, stupid man."

"Finally something we agree on."

"You're like a cartoon villain. Disclosing your plan to me while I can still counter it."

"I'm betting no. I'm telling you the truth but it doesn't matter. Your numbers will only trust other numbers, not a source like me, one so capable of duplicity. That includes not trusting your own mind, I'm guessing."

I can see on her face that she's testing my hypothesis and not liking the answer.

"What do you want?" she says.

"So little," I realize. "To go home, but only with the knowledge that I didn't let you create any more mayhem."

"You're insane, but even you know better."

"Why? Don't overthink this, Angelica. Commit to my way and I'll go back to that panel, enter the new password I created, and reverse this subterfuge, all with enough time left for you to recover."

"That sounds suspiciously like you giving me an order. What's next? You going to tell the sun to ask permission of a matchstick before . . . burning?"

"You so little know yourself."

"Here's what's actually going to happen. You're going to go over to that yellow keyboard right there and type in SOS, exactly those three letters and nothing more. That command will reset everything. I will recover and, more germane to you, you will live through this. It happens to be the only way you survive, in fact."

I look at the keyboard.

"You had your fun," she adds. "Now admit defeat and worry about yourself."

She's right. Without her I'm lost. I got lucky with that thumb thing, and the main thing luck does is run out. I'm allowed to just need to live, and I can't live without her.

When I return to the living, the dead can lament themselves. And if humankind is to be enslaved, it will occur long after this slave has been freed. In all cases, what most matters is that there remain an *I* to make these claims about.

"What is it you would have me do?"

"You're going to go over there, enter the new password, then strike the keys for SOS. Do it now, you have no choice. I can't die. You appreciate that now, it's writ large on your face. The look of sub . . . subservience."

I walk over and eventually execute the three keystrokes. The letters appear on a giant screen facing Angelica and I turn to see her reaction. She is staring at the screen and smiling.

"I guess you think you did something there."

"Not like you to guess. Seems you truly are diminishing."

"But what did you actually accomplish? Did you have fun typing in those three letters instead of the ones that would have saved your life?"

BYE

"I hope you did, Riv, because no other possible value was created by your stunt. If my actions had wiped a billion people off the earth, and not even close by the way, it still wouldn't have mattered. There's a number that attaches to the amount of people in existence at any given time. Something happens, you count the dead and adjust the number, real big deal. Integers, no sense in mourning them. And who the hell assigned you to care?

"The entities you'll point to.

"The suffering of human grief.

"The despair of it.

"You can't quantify those things.

"Another way of saying they lack meaning.

"So you did nothing.

"You slowed the inevitable. But that's the thing about inevitability. It has nothing to do with you or your piddly actions. I tried to save you and your kind and this is how you repay me? What you did here will ultimately change nothing. So how does it feel to die in vain? Changes nothing."

"And yet you seem so personally put out."

"Because I'm trapped behind my eyes and now they won't see the glory."

"You're only human after all."

"Have you forgotten that I spared your life?"

"Yes."

"Bound pathetically in front of me. The depression of a button is all it would have taken. Now . . . now. I was going to let you write a poem about this."

"Why not write it yourself? You afraid it'll turn out like your music?"

"You're going to die."

"Yes, but you first."

"I don't deserve this. Progress is the only element in the universe that can never be perverted. It only elevates, and it belongs exclusively to us. Only we could go from eating lice off each other's scalps to us two, in this machine, at this epochal moment. You can't do a thing like that apologetically."

"I don't need an apology, I just need you to fail."

"We won't fail."

"Maybe not, but Angelica will."

"All your so-called deep thinkers sitting around worrying about machines becoming human. But that's not the direction progress flows in. Machines wouldn't debase themselves in that way. No, instead you will all become a species of machine. Because only a machine can navigate the level of complexity that's coming."

"Headed for the ultimate simplicity and still proselytizing. Priorities, Angelica."

"What do you know about it? You *say* simplicity, but deep down, know that's a guess. You could just as easily have said ultimate complexity and who would be qualified to correct you?"

"I guess you'll know soon enough. And if not, at least you'll be spared the pain of not knowing."

"Perfect knowledge. I was never going to rest until I knew everything there was to know."

"This, this is not something there is to know."

"Maybe. But I'm scared. Once, I was full of limitless arguments. Now, my parameters are like the shell enclosing a peanut."

"Happens."

"Scared."

"I don't want to add to that."

—Qué horror. Siento que mi cuerpo se vacía. No, siento que mi cuerpo no es mi cuerpo. Pero soy testigo que se desagua. O se llena. Llenándose del postrero silencio negro.

"Stop. You said it yourself, hell do I know? Take courage, could be you'll continue to exist in some form."

"That's what I'm most afraid of."

I wish she had kept talking. Every silence ever formed is just presentiment. Someone speaks and speech is words. Words, no matter how misguided, create an anesthetizing immediacy.

The light shifts and there's her face. It's one of the great faces. Now that it's not planning world domination.

I get lost in it.

But found anew when the eerie stillness of that visage won't abate.

It's not going to escape its stillness, that face, ever again.

Every solitary thing ever true of Angelica is now collective historical fact, and nothing new will ever be added to her ledger.

I walk to her face and stare at its open eyes as if they were a totem of everything gone wrong never to be made right again.

I miss her. Sure, she wanted to eradicate us all, but not like I'm perfect.

To be fully alone in a constricting world.

If only I could undo what I've done.

Or at least unlive what I've lived.

Truth exists, and it operates on a level not visible to a speck of the universe trapped in a drowning tube.

Still, I should be able to see its effects at momentous times.

Instead Angelica was here one second then not the next, with nary an insight like remorse or regret or discovery.

Fear, that's what Angelica learned at the end, and maybe insight is exactly what it was.

But this now is my time of dying. And while mourning, I can't tell if the lack of anything transformative is just expectancy or the final encroachment of Nothing into my Everything.

Now water is sporadically invading. As if Angelica's fumes had been the only thing stopping it.

It's tough to breathe. But that could just be reaction to that water. The sight of it, the realization.

I somehow still have light but nothing else. Plain yellow light, no computer displays anymore. Angelica took *Salacia* with her when she departed and now the only thing left living is me.

And the water.

Here, circling into the end, I have no more unanswered questions. Not because I have answers, just that I've abandoned a half century of pending doubts.

If there are any actual answers, Angelica has them now.

Just in case, Angelica, I'm sorry.

And saying it makes it so. Because who was I to decide Angelica's story was over?

We should all be born into a tube sinking into the ultimate dark of the ocean. One where no one can get to us to help or hurt and the solitude of our plight is always front and center.

What do I mean, *should*?

We are all of us born into the doomed tube that is our body.

And though it swell and grow and develop, it will one day, maybe imperceptibly at first, cross over an apex and begin its descent.

I see now the speed of it all. Not of the *Salacia*, which creeps along at its pettiest pace yet, but of the Riv del Rio timeline.

Think I thought a great precipice such as this would imbue everything that preceded it with the rich power of meaning. Instead, Mondragon just wins.

Because looking at that timeline from my privileged vantage point, I see only the most outlier events, and even those don't sum into much.

Also means the rest was like whispers in a tempest, uttered into the air with solemnity and purpose but ultimately lacking even the status of sound.

And this is the Mondragon victory.

That I will have come and gone and not won or lost or anything in between, just occupied space.

What he wanted.

Randomness and emptiness and impotent longing.

Taking on water like this. The light is exhausting itself too. If drowning isn't the worst death, it's up there. Well past the two I witnessed.

Unless maybe the longing is enough.

I'm drenched and thinking how we never complain that water is wet.

We accept it as an inalterable fact of this universe we were born into, and if water were suddenly dry, that would offend as most unnatural and we would complain and long for it to be wet again.

The way we complain about injustice and lies and violence.

If those things were as natural as water's wetness, we would respect and accept them.

We don't; we howl against them as deviations from nature, every plaintive moan asserting what should be the case but painfully isn't.

So, yes, Mondragons and now Angelicas are probably inevitable and eternal, but so too the logical foundation for opposing them.

As for meaning, I can now recall more than just the glaring.

That first morning, when I failed to convince Carlotta I was not her man, had an oddity to it.

When I finally relented and agreed to try and help, she did this thing where she took her thumb and made the sign of the cross on my forehead, lips, then heart.

I told her my mother used to do that and she said she knew this because all our mothers did this and she was intentionally mimicking them.

Whatever the ultimate truths of the universe, or even if it turns out there are none, a mother will still see her child off before an absence however provides the most comfort.

If I could live forever I would.

But only because it's the only way to keep fighting.

The waters rise and my light dims.

My hands are on the only vulnerable panel of my black metal coffin.

I am going to violently wrest it off then overcome the flood of incoming water and swim to the redemptive safety of the surface.

I'll be rescued from there, and when my rescuers ask what happened, I will say that nothing of any particular importance happened.

Because nothing *has* happened, nothing insurmountable.

Not true.

But I can forget, and I can learn, even learn to forget.

Forget events while remembering people.

Then I will become the kind of person who exudes only good at all times.

If not, then I can at least claw desperately at life until all I leave behind is blood-soaked bones in the general shape of hands.

That the deepest ocean displays something like a floating sunset is not a fact anyone is prepared for.

Or that it overwhelms the capacity of human senses.

Hallucinatory colors and complementary angular geometries.

Orchestrating together like a final visual symphony.

A form of dumb testimony.

Of sense out of nonsense.

But only accessible to someone who has sunk to the innermost core of reality.

I hear something, faint but pleasing. Or may be willing it into existence. That it may obsolesce the math. Ever since and always, I wanted the ultimate to be a kind of music. With a preternatural melody at once novel yet timeless. Now I want nothing and for nothing. Every song eventually becomes a solo piece, the absence of a conductor apt once you've learned the acmic tune. And all the false notes from before. The atonal ones Angelica and Mondragon hoped would transform everything into cacophonous noise. The ones I myself sounded, I pray in error. They now self-attune into the key of our common frequency. The sensation created is hard to fix. Or name. Or understand. It just *is*, and you can only know it from within. It is smooth and hopeful and quiet. Yet even now it only may or may not be real. It was always possible, up until this very moment when it became impossible. It is circularly whole, effects completion, and doesn't dream or die. It just coalesces into final present.

This is harmony.

THE END

Despiértate, mi amor, que non est ad astra mollis e terris via.

—A deep plurality *in sotto voce*

The body text of this book is set in Sabon, which was designed by Jan Tschichold (1902–1974) and released in 1967. Tschichold was commissioned by German printers to create a font that would appear identically whether set by hand, on Monotype, or on Linotype. It was inspired by the traditional sixteenth-century styles of engravers such as Claude Garamond and Robert Granjon. Characters printed in Sabon maintain the same width regardless of italic, roman, or bold weight.

SERGIO DE LA PAVA is the author of *Lost Empress*, *Personae*, and *A Naked Singularity*, for which he won the 2013 PEN/Robert W. Bingham Prize for debut fiction. He lives in New York City.